From the Shadows

By

E.L.Bates

Copyright © 2015 E.L. Bates

All rights reserved. No part of this publication may be reproduced or retransmitted in any form, or by any means, without written permission.

ISBN-10: 0-9899551-2-5
ISBN-13: 978-0-9899551-2-6

FIRST EDITION

Cover design by Fly Casual

stardancepress.com

Part One

Thursday, April 23, 2016/I've no idea what this universe's dating system is.

I woke up in a coffin.

I screamed. Nobody but a vampire ever really expects such a thing.

I banged and clawed and desperately tried to see or feel something, anything, that would get me out.

(In retrospect, really glad that didn't happen, or I would be dead and in a *real* coffin now.)

Andrew once accidentally shut me in our huge, walk-in closet the first year we were married, and I went ballistic. There was still plenty of room to move around, but he'd turned off the light and closed the door, forgetting I was in there (we were such newlyweds, we kept being startled by the fact that we were living with another person) until I started to scream. That was the first time either of us realized the depth of my claustrophobia.

This was so much worse. I couldn't even raise my arms above my head; all my scratching and pounding had to happen at my sides. The top of the container didn't quite touch my face, but it was close enough I could sense it, right above me. My legs and feet were firmly pinned.

I don't know how long I was in there. Long enough to move from panic, to hyperventilating, to the one tiny part of my brain that always remains functional no matter how bad everything else gets whispering I would die right then and there if I didn't get a grip on myself, to numb horror interspersed with moments of squirming and screaming again, in hopes that this time, I'd be able to get free.

I never even questioned why I was there, didn't ask how I went from falling asleep on my couch to waking up in a grave. I didn't consider for one second that it was a nightmare. I know nightmares, they've been my close companions for a year. This was all too real, and it didn't matter how it had happened, all that mattered was making it stop.

It was in one of my hopelessly quiet stretches that *something* grabbed my coffin and dragged it around. From within my metal womb, it felt like a giant hand lifting me—or no, not a hand, more like a giant dog snatching me up in its mouth and shaking me to and fro. Naturally I started screaming again, only this time it wasn't just because of terror, I actually hoped there was someone around to hear. Even if it was a beast.

When I had to pause to drag in a gasping, sobbing breath, I heard voices. And then my coffin went *clangggg!* and landed on something hard.

Then, at last, I could hear and feel through the surrounding metal hands scrambling to get the lid off. They lifted it up, and I promptly thought I was going to die again. The light that streamed in was so bright, it sliced through my eyes and went straight to my brain.

I was too hoarse to scream anymore at that point. I think I let loose with a weak "Augh!" as I flung myself desperately out of the coffin, tipped over the side, and landed in a huddle on the cold, hard metal floor with my arms flung around my head.

I hadn't even managed one glimpse of my rescuers.

They tugged on me a bit, and babbled in my ears, but I was concentrating on not throwing up and not exposing my eyes to the light, and managed to ignore them. What seemed like dozens of voices fired off questions in various languages. At last I heard, in English, a precise voice saying, "Do you understand this?"

I managed a nod, though how they saw me do it through my arms and hands protecting my face I'm not sure. A new voice cut through all the rest, and I couldn't help but listen to him.

"For goodness' sake, you idiots, back off and give her some room! Henderson, dim the lights, can't you see it's too bright? You'd be screaming in pain too if some moron exposed your eyes to bright light after being in the dark for 500 years." His words were angry, but his voice was beautiful, a deep baritone with the slightest hint of a burr underneath it. Even at that moment, with my stomach trying to heave itself out my mouth, I thought he'd make a fantastic singer.

Then one hand gently rested on my shoulder, in direct contrast to the many hands pushing and prodding me moments before.

"Don't worry," he said, and now that lovely voice was a gentle purr. "Take your time. We've turned down the lights. There's no rush. When you feel ready, go ahead and open your eyes. You're safe here. No one is going to hurt you. We want to help. I know you're confused. We're a little puzzled ourselves. It's going to be all right. We'll all figure this out together."

I cautiously lowered my arms and blinked once, quickly. When my vision didn't explode into starbursts of pain, I opened my eyes fully.

Squatting in front of me, with his hand on my shoulder still, was the man with the Voice. I had to blink a few more times to get the tears clear, but then, at last, I could make out details.

He was a big guy, that much was obvious even when he was resting on his heels. Big shoulders, big chest, really tall ... not surprising, given how deep his voice was. His face was ordinary—I'd half expected him to be breathtakingly handsome, to match his voice, but he was pretty plain, really. Not ugly, but nothing to write home about. Brown eyes, brown hair, pale skin that seemed to have an almost blue tint to it—at first I hazily thought he must be cold, but then I figured it was just the dim lighting playing tricks on my eyes. Appearance-wise, maybe about five years older than me, but I'd always been lousy at guessing people's ages by their face.

"All right?" he asked.

Not even close, but since I figured he was talking about my vision, I managed a nod.

"Do you know who you are?"

That was a weird question—why wouldn't I?—but also an easy one. "Riss—uh, Nerissa Waldon," I croaked, then clamped my mouth shut again. I was *really* nauseous, way more than could be accounted for by the claustrophobia.

"Do you have any idea where you are?"

I shook my head once, not daring to try to speak again.

A new voice entered our conversation, the one that had first spoken to me in English. He moved closer, but didn't bend down so I could see his face. Jerk. I had a lovely view of his shiny brown boots, though.

"You are aboard my ship," he said, his words clipped and his "r"s strongly pronounced, with not quite an English accent but almost.

I muzzily thought of boats and oceans, and wondered why, if I was on a ship, I couldn't hear any waves splashing against the side, feel any rocking, or smell salt in the air. For some reason, I had thought we were in some kind of warehouse. I guessed that I could be on a really huge ship, or even a submarine, but—

"Your pod was part of a convoy of a dozen biochemically frozen individuals we came across, floating in space," Not-English Guy continued. "Yours alone showed signs of life. We brought your pod in and released you."

Biochemically frozen? Like the ad I'd seen last week? Wait—did he say *space*?

I had kept my head down-ish this entire time, not willing to risk puking by looking up, but I couldn't bear it any longer. I sat upright on my knees and looked around.

We *were* in a room that looked like a warehouse, big and square-ish and utilitarian. Filling most of it was a really weird plane/rocket thing. Andrew might have been able to tell what it was just by looking, but it was beyond me. Next to it, looking really small and horrible, was my shiny silver coffin, what Not-English Guy had called my pod (Scottish! my brain filled in. He was Scottish—or his voice was, at least). Filling in the rest of the empty space between those items and me were people.

Scottish Guy had a gorgeous, sculptured face, golden-brown with sharp cheekbones and a chiseled jaw and piercing black eyes. His hair was black, too, and looked like it might have been curly if he let it grow a little bit more. If I'd seen him before hearing him speak, I would have guessed he was from India or a Middle Eastern country—which I suppose he still could have been, ethnically. His firm mouth was set in a definite frown as he stared down at me.

Then I couldn't look at him anymore, because all the other people in the room grabbed my attention. A stunningly beautiful black woman, watching me with an unreadable expression; an Asian girl with her hand resting on a weird-looking gun holstered at her hip (that freaked me out more than a little); this guy who looked like one of Tolkien's elves, with pointed ears, paper-white skin, weird vertical ridges on his cheeks, and long, flowing locks of shiny blond hair (he had to be in costume, right, even though that would be weird?); a woman with really black skin, I mean *black*, not the dark African or West Indian coloring we call black, and *four arms*; a fairly ordinary-looking older guy with grey hair and cold blue eyes set in a tanned face; and a man with shimmering silver skin (literally, it kept catching the light and sparkling) and lively golden eyes, with a huge grin on his face like this was the most fun he'd had in ages.

I think it was the four arms that did me in. I dove for my coffin but didn't quite make it before I threw up all over the floor. Beautiful Voice followed me, ordering the others to stay back in his grumpy tone again. He didn't pat my shoulder or rub my back, which I would have hated, but he pulled my hair away from my face and silently waited for me to finish emptying my guts.

"I don't understand any of this," I finally stammered, stuffing my humiliation at throwing up in front of so many strangers, even if half of them were freaks, firmly down where it wouldn't interfere with what was important right now. "Last night I went to sleep on the couch in my apartment, like I always do. When I woke up, I was in there." I waved at the pod, then moved away from my sickness and sat shakily on the floor.

Beautiful Voice sat down next to me, bringing his knees up in front of him and resting his hands on them. "You didn't join any program in the year 2016 to be biochemically frozen and sent into space for—"

"Settling of new, terraformed worlds once we'd developed enough to do that sort of thing?" I finished for him. "No. I saw the ad, but I didn't sign up. I thought the whole thing was bizarre." I wasn't about to tell strangers how tempted I had been, how appealing the idea of sleeping for a few hundred years and then waking up to start a brand new life away from my family and the shards of my old life had been to me. I had never really considered it seriously (though a few more phone calls from my sisters might have changed that), but the advertisement *was* tempting, even if in the end I decided it was insanity.

"Good instincts," said the stunning woman (the one who was African-type black, not the four-armed Really-Black one).

I was starting to be able to look at the obviously not-human people without my insides wanting to shrivel. Not that any of them were hideous, but my brain just kept screaming at me that they were *wrong*, they were impossible.

I've always loved fantasy and sci-fi, especially space opera. I think all those books and TV shows and movies allowed me to start reasoning through what I was seeing and what Beautiful Voice and Scottish Guy were saying, and to piece it together. I've always been good at puzzles, fitting together weird bits to make the big picture make sense.

"You're from the future. My future," I said.

Beautiful Voice nodded, his eyebrows going up like he was impressed.

"And I was somehow floating in space with the people who signed up for bio-freezing. Even though I didn't do that. And ... you said none of them survived, but somehow I did. And woke up from the freezing, which I didn't do but obviously must have because I couldn't have survived in a coffin in space for however many years, all on my own, before you guys showed up. And then you grabbed my coffin with some sort of tractor beam or space grappling hook, and now I'm on your ... spaceship. Starship. Imperial cruiser. Whatever you call it." I covered my mouth with my hand as the desire to puke surged again.

"The nausea is a side effect of awakening from the bio-freeze," Beautiful Voice informed me, the professional tone settling his role firmly in my mind. This guy had to be the ship's doctor. It made sense, the way he was making sure I was all right and how he bossed everyone else around.

That meant that Scottish Guy had to be the captain. I looked at him again. He still seemed annoyed, and not at all impressed by my brilliant logic. Which, considering that I could have been screaming and panicking instead of sitting there talking mostly-calmly about it, kind of bugged me.

"We call it a space-going vessel," he informed me now. "Spaceship will do. A space corvette belonging to the Alliance Exploratory Forces, to be specific. *Not* a passenger vessel."

"It was a really bad plan," Stunning Woman said, ignoring this. "The bio-freezing and terraforming," she clarified. "About a hundred years after they did the freezing, technology finally advanced to where they could send the ships out. Except they didn't have any planet for them to land on yet, just proof that there were such planets. So they sent out the ship anyway, manned by computers, with instructions to land on the first terraformable planet it came across, and unfreeze the people once there, so that they could begin the process of transforming the planet to make it livable. Hard to imagine anything going wrong with such a brilliant, foolproof plan as that, isn't there?" Her mouth turned up on one side, and despite everything, a smile tried to quiver around my mouth in response.

"It didn't work," she continued. "The ship vanished from their sensors almost immediately. Nobody could ever find any trace of it, until Ru El here," she nodded to Elf-Guy, "picked up your life signs in the middle of the debris field way out here in deep space, and then we put two and two together. We didn't expect that you been part of the trip without ever, you know, having been part of it."

Elf-Guy—Ru El, as she called him, spoke in a misty, far-away voice. "By your reckoning, it is the year 2526. You have been asleep for 510 years. So very strange."

Time travel, bio-freezing, mysterious abduction from my own couch, aliens and spaceships. I grabbed my head with both hands.

"And here comes the headache," said Beautiful Voice. "Another side effect from the freezing. Come on, Nerissa," he said, standing up and holding his hand out to me. "Let's get you to sickbay."

He and Silver-Skin Dude hustled me down the corridors (cream and brown, rounded walls, and would have been utterly fascinating if my head hadn't felt like Athena was trying to burst forth from it fully grown) to the sickbay, a room full of beds and clear cases and weird instruments, and then Doctor Beautiful Voice pumped me full of drugs. I dozed off for a while, and when I woke up he'd brought me my journal, rescued from the shuttle bay by Silver-Skin Dude. I fell asleep last night with it in my hands. It's brand-new, I bought it in hopes it would inspire me to start writing poetry and songs again. I tried writing last night—or 510 years ago—but my emotions were too much for me. I'd fallen asleep with it in my hands, thinking about Andrew and all the events of the past year, but unable to get any of them out. It must have transferred to the pod with me.

I'm so glad to have it. Not only does it give me a place to record all these bizarre things happening to me, it's a little piece of home, some proof that I haven't turned into a character in a movie, but am still Riss.

"Thank you," I said, stammering a little over the lump in my throat. "And thank—whatever his name is, the, um, person who got it out of the pod."

"Chief Petty Officer Tyler," Doctor Beautiful Voice said. "Well, his real name is something like *Ty'le'rehonorogh'mumblemumtle*, but he allows everyone to call him Tyler. He's our Chief Engineer."

At this point, I opened up my journal and started jotting down notes so I could keep people straight. "And, uh, he's not human?"

A hint of a smile quirked the corners of the doctor's mouth. "No." He cleared his throat. "My name's Selby, by the way. If you're keeping track. Gideon Selby, chief medical officer aboard this ship. And for the record, I myself am only half human."

I tried to keep my jaw from dropping; Roz always says—said—that makes me look like a halfwit. "That explains the blueish skin then," I said, striving for a neutral tone.

He nodded. "My mother's people are completely blue, with black markings covering their entire bodies. I've just got the patterns on my arms and legs." He obligingly rolled up his sleeves, and sure enough, black swirls and dots danced up and down his arms, just touching his wrists, looking like the most elegant tattoos I'd ever seen.

"I ... see," I said. I industriously wrote this down as well, mostly in hopes that the writing of it would make it seem more real (it hasn't, not yet. Maybe *reading* it, and filling in more details as I go, will. One can hope). "And the others?"

Doctor Selby rested his hip against the corner of his desk. "The Captain is one Arthur Miles. Wholly human."

And wholly has a stick up his rear, I thought but didn't say aloud. I don't think Dr. Selby is the type to idolize his captain, but one never knows.

"His first mate is Commander Sapphira Osei-Koné, also wholly human."

"Which one was she?"

"The one who talked to you about the bio-freezing."

Stunning Woman, then. Not the four-armed one or the jittery gun-toting one. Well, the "wholly human" bit probably ruled out the four-armed one anyway, but hey, for all I knew, they had made some crazy genetic advances in the last 500 years. 500 years! *Anything* could have happened. Spaceships and aliens and time travel, oh my.

"Who was the four-armed woman?"

"Our navigator, Adele Vreean. As you might have guessed, not human. From the planet Driiviia, in fact. She tells our helmsman where to fly the ship."

"And the helmsman is …?"

"Ru El. Of Koloth. He was the one with the pointy ears and lovely blond locks."

Not an elf. Not that I really believe in elves in space, but given everything else that's happened, "believe" and "not believe" are starting to blend together.

"And that just leaves Lieutenant Natalie Christensen, our head of security. Human," Selby added.

That must have been the jittery gun girl. It explained the jitters and the gun—until I came out of the pod and started talking, nobody here would have had no idea if I was hostile or friendly.

I rubbed my head again. Dr. Selby took note.

"I think it's time for you to get some sleep, Nerissa," he said.

"Just let me write a little bit more," I pleaded. Seriously, if I didn't get all this down, how would I remember?

He loomed over me with a scowl. "Five minutes, and then you must sleep, or I'm taking it away."

I finished filling this out more quickly than I've ever written anything in my life.

So concludes today's adventures. I'm not sure I'm ready to think about tomorrow's yet.

Friday, April 24, 2016/I know it's not really, but how else am I supposed to keep track of how much time I've spent here?

Woke up this morning with only a lingering dry mouth and tiny ache behind my eyes left over from bio-freezing. Whatever else the future has going for it, its medicine sure has improved.

Dr. Selby called in Sapphira as soon as I'd woken up (Commander Osei-Koné, really, but she told me to call her Sapphira, since I'm not in AEF, aka the Alliance Exploratory Forces), and she helped me shower and get dressed in some new clothes. They aren't really new, but they're clean and new to me, and I asked her to pass on my profuse thanks to whomever was lending her off-duty wardrobe to me.

I also thanked Dr. Selby for thinking of it in the first place. I don't think I could have eaten breakfast or done anything while I was still in my old t-shirt and yoga pants. They stank of sweat and puke and terror, and if it hadn't been for the drugs I never would have been able to sleep in them last night.

He looked surprised that I thanked him, but it meant a lot that he understood, without me having to say anything, how important it was to me to be clean.

The clothing isn't too wildly bizarre to me—thankfully, styles haven't evolved to include bared breasts or anything else that would make me blush to see and most especially to wear. It reminds me faintly of styles of the Ancient World, only, you know, futuristic instead of ancient. At least, what I've got on now and what I've so far seen is. Who knows what alien styles are like.

(I wonder if we call them aliens now? Dr. Selby just said "not human" when describing them to me last night, but he might have been doing that to keep it simple for me. Are humans the dominant species in the galaxy, and therefore everyone else called aliens, like in the shows? Or is there another dominant species, and so then are humans part of the "alien" designator? Or does each species just call others aliens to themselves, or something else that hasn't even occurred to me?)

Anyway, I'm wearing a soft thigh-length structured purple tunic with ¾ sleeves split down the center and ruffled along the edges and cuffs, and dark blue pants that feel like really comfortable stretch pants but look more like dressy skinny jeans. No seams on any of them, which boggles the mind. How are they made? I've no boots or shoes or even socks, so I'm still barefoot. Thankfully it's a comfortable temperature in here, and I never mind going barefoot when it's warm.

Even clean underwear and bra, and these are way cool. I mean, just ordinary in style, but how they're created ... Sapphira handed me a little tube and explained that you spray it. I said ?????

So basically, you push a button on the tube while pointing at the parts you want covered, and out comes this black goo which sticks and then spreads and thins and adapts to your skin color, and hardens after a few moments into a flexible, barely-noticeable covering which just *stays on*. When you want to change it you peel it off and drop it in a bin, where it is cleaned and broken back down into its original form, and then pumped back into tubes to be reused.

Like I said, *way cool*. Even if my first attempt covered my stomach and thighs instead of the, er, proper areas. I have lousy aim, OK? The second attempt worked, at least.

After all the excitement of getting dressed I had breakfast, which was not exciting, just a plastic-y tray with gross scrambled eggs and dry toast and some sort of citrus fruit. Hospital food is hospital food no matter what century it is, I guess.

Sapphira had to go back to her duties after showing me how to work the shower and the underthings, but she said she'd be back later to talk some more and we'd try to get more details of what happened to me figured out, and see if there's any way to send me back. Time travel is crazy hard, pretty much impossible, from what she said, but there are weird quirks to it, so we might be able to do something.

Dr. Selby is looking at the results from my blood-work and frowning. I'd be worried, except I'm already starting to figure out that a frown is his most common expression. Apparently, according to Sapphira, when Dr. Selby is kind to you, that's when you start to worry, because you know you're in bad shape.

Oh, who am I kidding. I am completely freaked out inside. What's wrong with my tests? Am I going to start aging rapidly, 500 years in just a few days, or did the bio-freezing screw something else up inside me, or what?

I'm trying to be calm and rational about everything, and even enjoy the adventure—because what's the point in having an impossible time-travel space adventure if you spend all of it in a screaming panic?—but it's a lot harder than I would have expected. Not that I ever did expect anything like this, of course. Who would?

I miss Andrew. Not like I haven't been missing him every day for a year and a day now, but I wish so much he were here with me. He thought sci-fi was stupid, but tolerated it for my sake, and he'd be very, very firm and calm and "We'll figure this out" and "Don't talk down to my wife, Captain Stick-up-your-Rear; just because she's small doesn't mean she's stupid" and no matter what happened, it would be OK because we'd be together.

Dammit. Crying now.

Later.

I was completely mortified to burst into tears in front of Dr. Selby, but he was great about it. He didn't make a big fuss, just came and brought me a handkerchief-type thing (made out of the same material as the underclothes) and a tube of water and stood by in case I wanted anything. When I flapped my hands at him, he correctly interpreted that as "Thanks, I'm good " (actually, it was more like "Go away forever, I hate everyone," but I tried to tone my flaps down since I knew deep down none of this was his fault) and went back to his test results until I was done.

Then he looked up and said, "Anything you want to talk about?"

"No," I said, and blew my nose one final time. And I didn't.

After Andrew died, everyone in my family tried to force me to talk about my *feeelings*. "Don't hold it in, Rissy, you'll make yourself sick. It's OK to cry in front of your family. We love you. Just talk to us. You don't want to shut everyone out."

They seemed to completely forget that ever since I was a kid, I preferred to work through my emotions alone. Or no, they didn't forget. They never bothered to pay attention. Andrew knew better. And because he respected me enough to leave me alone when I said that's what I wanted, eventually I grew to be able to take comfort from him and be with him even in the midst of sorrow or other strong reactions. Until he died and I was back on my own, trying to hold my ground against the force of my family trying make me into something I'm not.

Dr. Selby didn't try to force me to talk, either. He nodded his head when I said no, and went back to what he was doing. Then he paused and said,

"Sorry, should have been clearer. Anything you want to talk about with someone other than me? Sapphira's on duty, but I can get someone else in here, someone decent at being comforting and saying 'There, there' if you'd like."

That actually made me laugh. "Really, I'm—well, I'm not fine, obviously, and it would be stupid to claim I am, but I don't need to talk. To anyone."

And that was that.

He just now dropped a comb on the table next to my bed. I thanked him again, and he looked shocked again that I would do so. Is thanking out of style in this century? It's weird that they all look so taken aback every time I say thanks for something.

Time to stop writing and work some of these tangles out of my hair. Sapphira obviously understands curly hair, because the stuff she gave me to clean it kept it from frizzing like it usually does after a shampoo, but it's going to be a matted rats' nest if I don't put some effort in now.

Sapphira's hair is gorgeous, these tight, natural curls that are completely wild all around her head and are kept back from her face with a wide, soft, cream-colored band. I seriously think she's the most beautiful woman I've ever seen. Not just because her features are so pretty, but because she exudes this confidence and authority, like she's never had a moment of self-doubt in her life.

She looks like she's right around my age, early thirties. Wish I could borrow some of that confidence. *And* some of her hair mojo, because I've been trying for the last five minutes to work out one snarl, and it hurt so much I had to put the comb down and write this about Sapphira before trying again.

Ow!

* * *

Friday, Later Again.

Sapphira came back to sickbay after lunch and hair-wrangling. (I put it in one fat braid so that I won't have to mess with it again for a while. Not as stylish as springy curls hanging down past my shoulders, but it's not like I'm trying to attract anybody, and I have a sneaking suspicion that efficiency is considered more attractive than anything else aboard the ship.) Sapphira said she was just off bridge duty, and wanted to answer as many of my questions as possible.

"I thought," she said with a mostly-straight face, "that you might appreciate some polysyllabic answers."

"I heard that," the Doc said.

I managed a smile. After a shower and two meals, I was feeling much more like myself. Still overwhelmed, but ready to take some interest in the adventure that has swept me up.

"I have so many questions I don't even know where to start," I said, trying not to flap my hands while I spoke. "Maybe you could just give me some basics?" I brandished my journal. "And do you mind if I take notes?"

Sapphira sat down on the corner of my bed. "Sure. You are on board the AEF space corvette *Caledonia*, for starters."

"Not the Good Ship *Lollipop*, then," I murmured. "How disappointing."

Dr. Selby, ostensibly working at his desk, snorted. I decided to count that as a small victory.

Sapphira followed my eyes to the doctor and chuckled. "We are on a deep space exploratory mission, which is exactly what it sounds like. We are pushing the boundaries of space and of our technology, mapping and exploring and hopefully finding new planets and peoples to join the Alliance." Her eyes glowed as she spoke, and her entire body straightened with pride and passion.

"How long are you going to be gone from Earth?" I asked. "Or wherever the Alliance's headquarters are."

"Ten years." Sapphira answered. "Five years out, and five years back. We've been gone for two years already. And yes, we left from Earth."

"Oh," I said faintly.

"That's some of why Captain Miles is so unhappy about you being here," Dr. Selby spoke up from his corner. "It's not you personally so much as it is the interference with the mission. The best thing to do would be to take you back to Earth or Arethra and let the scientists there figure out how you got here and if t's possible to send you back, but we can't do that without scrapping the entire mission. So it's either get you home ourselves or have you aboard for the next eight years."

Ye gods.

"What, uh, what exactly is the Alliance Exploratory Fleet?" I asked quickly, in hopes of distracting myself.

"Exactly what it sounds like," Sapphira answered. "We are the government's official explorers and adventurers."

I took a few moments to scribble this down, still stunned by the whole *eight years in space* idea. If they couldn't get me home ...

More questions seemed in order, if only to distract myself.

"How long has the Alliance been around? And is it ..." I trailed off, not sure how to ask if it was benevolent or oppressive in a non-insulting manner.

Sapphira laughed. "Time for a crash course in history! The short version: about a hundred years ago, Earth finally made enough technological advances to be able to venture beyond our own galaxy. That's where we met our first alien-to-us species, the Arethrans."

"My mother's people," Dr. Selby said.

"They were at about the same place technologically as Earth, and so the two planets formed an alliance."

"And that was it?" I asked. I'm not sure what I'd expected, but this part of history was boringly tame.

Sapphira nodded. "A few years later, the people of the planet Koloth petitioned to join the Alliance. They were at war with another planet in the same system, and losing."

Even in the future, it seems, no advances can be made without bloodshed. So much for utopia.

"Over the next forty years, the Alliance continued to grow as other planets joined. There were a few small wars, but it eventually grew into a time of peace, which is when the AEF was formed. Two years ago, to commemorate the 100th anniversary of the Alliance, *Caledonia* was commissioned as the first AEF ship solely dedicated to exploring and mapping space, as well as seeking to expand the Alliance in a peaceful manner."

It was better than I had expected. If I had to get catapulted into the future, to land on a spaceship in the middle of nowhere, this wasn't so bad. At least they aren't going around acting like they are superior to everyone else, or actively trying to conquer all other worlds.

A shiny box on Sapphira's belt beeped. I tried not to stare too obviously, in case it was something personal, but when Sapphira plucked the box free and held it to her mouth, I decided it was a personal communicator of some sort, and I was free to gawk.

"Osei-Koné," Sapphira said crisply.

The words that came through sounded garbled to my ears, something like: "Bridge you must *gibberish* at once come *gibberish*. Planet *gibberish* been sighted has."

"My way on," Sapphira answered, then reattached the box to her belt. "Sorry, Nerissa, the rest of this will have to wait. The probes have discovered a planet, and I'm needed on the bridge for our reversion to real-space." A grin split her face. "After two years of dullness, first a mysterious visitor from the past, and now our first unknown planet!"

"Oh good, new diseases for me to have to treat," Dr. Selby muttered as she rushed out.

I stared at the door that vanished as Sapphira approached it and reappeared again as soon as she passed through. "What *language* was that?" I asked.

"Oh." Selby paused. "Of course you wouldn't recognize that. It's the trade language, a patois of sorts formed of Arethran, English, Chinese, and Spanish. It's the common tongue of the Alliance."

"Does that mean I'm not going to be able to talk to most people?" I asked in dismay.

"The AEF Academy is located in Scotland—is there a Scotland in your time?" At my nod, he continued. "So all the officers aboard the ship speak English. And I would guess that you'll pick up the patois quickly enough just by listening. If you stay here long enough, that is."

I'm not sure whether to feel reassured or not by that. On the one hand, it's good to know I won't be barred from communicating with the crew of the ship by language difficulties. On the other, what do I feel about staying here long enough to have to develop my language skills? Eight years in space ...

"Or you could petition the captain for a translator," the Doctor added.

That sounded more promising than trying to learn a new language, even if part of it *was* my native tongue.

"He'll probably say no, though," Dr. Selby finished. "He doesn't like Alliance tech in non-Alliance hands. Or tentacles or ... whatever various species use to grasp."

So much for that.

This is all incredibly overwhelming, and even though I've done nothing at all today, I feel exhausted. It's one thing to wistfully and not-seriously-at-all think about letting yourself be frozen for hundreds of years and then start a new life. Turns out it's a completely different matter to have that decision wrenched from your hands and find yourself actually living it.

Friday, later yet.

Night cycle now. I'm tempted to get all dramatic and announce in a booming voice, "It's always night in space," but I am curbing my weirdness as much as possible. I'm under strict orders from Dr. Selby to sleep, but I managed to convince him that I'd sleep much better if I could write for a while first. He's given me a time limit, and if I show any signs of loopiness, I'm certain that time limit will expire at once. He may be a great physician and a kind man, but he is *bossy*.

I keep thinking about this mission. *Ten years.* I can't imagine volunteering to leave everyone and everything for that long. Granted, yes, I did imagine leaving behind my family and friends to do the bio-freezing, but despite the evidence, I didn't actually do it. And I never would have considered it had Andrew still been alive, or my family less ... themselves.

This crew is mostly single people, and there are a few married to each other, but there are some who have left spouses behind. Even children. I really cannot fathom that. It makes me almost angry to think about. My husband is gone forever and neither of us had a choice about it, and yet here are people willingly going away from their spouses, and for what? Just for the thrill of being able to say they were part of the first long-term, deep space mission? Give me a break.

I need to calm down. Dr. Selby is giving me the scowling side-eye. I suppose my heavy breathing and vise-like grip on the pen were giving away my rising emotions.

Ahem. Back to today.

The planet the ship's probes picked up is still a few days out, now that we're out of what they call "fold-space" and into "real-space." They are going to gather as much data as they can from said probes and long-range sensors until they reach orbit, at which point they will try to contact any people who live there, or, if it is uninhabited but able to be visited, send down a landing party to explore and map and learn as much as they can about it.

It would be so, so cool to be part of either of those scenarios, but I'm not holding out hope. I'm not part of the scientists onboard or the AEF crew, and I doubt either the captain or the head scientist would want to include me. I'm a nuisance to both of them.

The scientists are their own separate crew: geologists, astronomers, physicists, even some archeologists and anthropologists. These last two want to talk to me tomorrow and ask me all about Earth 500 years ago. Apparently I am the first person to ever successfully travel from the past to now or vice-versa without dying along the way. Go me.

The scientists are Alliance, but not part of the Fleet, and they follow the Captain's orders while on the ship but are autonomous once they're in a planetary scientific situation. It all sounds very ticklish to me, and it's no wonder why Captain Miles is a crank, even not accounting for his injury that booted him out of the navy and into the

AEF. Two bosses of two groups on one ship is rarely a good situation.

Speaking of the Captain and 500 years ago, Captain Miles contacted Earth almost as soon as I got hustled to sickbay yesterday to appraise them of the situation and ask for as much detail as they can possibly dig up about the bio-freeze project of five-freakin'-hundred years ago. I cannot get over that. 500 years! It's no wonder I feel a little loopy. Imagine if someone from the 1500s was suddenly transported to my day and age. Everything is different, from technology and clothing right down to ideologies and how people think and act. A folk musician aboard an exploring spaceship is as out-of-place as a wandering minstrel in a big corporation.

I wonder why they have ship people and science people, but no diplomatic people. If part of their goal is to form relationships with new species, you'd think they'd be equipped with ambassadors and diplomats as well. Captain Miles is clearly no diplomat! So who is in charge of establishing relations with other peoples, who makes sure nobody precipitates a war through cultural ignorance? That's not something that ought to be left to chance, I would think.

The head science dude is the bland grey-haired man from the shuttle bay yesterday when I arrived (that's what Sapphira said it is, and the weird plane/rocket thing is the shuttle). Dr. Selby forgot to tell me about him. His name is Dr. Eggleston, which is an absolute perfect name for a scholar if you ask me, and from the face Dr. Selby made and Sapphira tried not to make, I gather they really don't like him. Not exactly looking forward to meeting him.

The rest of the afternoon was a lot more tests and bloodwork, though Selby won't tell me why, just that he's covering all the bases. Super helpfu , Doc, thanks. I feel so reassured now. I've met the junior medical officer and the nurses and a bunch of other staff, but none of them have really talked to me, and I can't remember any of their names.

This is all *so weird*. Have I mentioned that? Because I think I'd have to mention it about a thousand times before it becomes clear just how weird it is. My brain still hasn't fully comprehended the fact that I'm in space, 500 years in the future, on a ship with aliens and humans combined, and nobody had a clue how I got here or how to get me back, or even if it's possible *to* get me back.

I want to go back. I do, really. This is a wild adventure, but I can't stay here for the rest of my life. Can I? Why am I even asking this, am I trying to convince myself? I can't possibly want to stay. Why should I?

Andrew is gone. I don't owe my family anything. I have friends, but ... I don't know. Maybe I could stay here forever.

Oh, get real, Riss. What could you do aboard this ship for the next eight years? A musician? In a style considered "quirky" even in your own time? And once the ship returned to Earth, what then, what would you do with the rest of your life? Of course I can't stay here. Of course all these clever science people are going to figure out how to send me home. Before long, I'll be back in my apartment, waking up on the couch, looking around and blinking, with only this journal to prove it wasn't a dream. It's crazy to think anything else.

The Doc is looming over me with a very threatening face. I gather my time for writing is up.

Saturday, April 25, 2016, or the Alliance equivalent.

Woke up screaming from a nightmare. Managed to pitch myself off the bed in my sleep, landed on the floor in a tangle of blankets. Scared the night crew in sickbay half to death. So mortified I can hardly stand it.

Dr. Selby was great. He was right there (doesn't that man ever go off duty?), helped me calm down, got fresh sheets on the bed, made me drink of cup of chamomile tea (mmm, hay flavor, my favorite—you'd think after 500 years they could have figured out a way to make chamomile taste less like dusty grass), and now he's—grumpily—letting me write this down in hopes I'll be able to sleep if I get it out of my system.

I dreamed I was back in the pod, trapped, screaming and trying to thrash and begging someone, anyone to open it and *let me out.* (I'm pretty sure I screamed that out loud—the Doc looked totally unsurprised when I mumbled something about claustrophobia.)

Then I managed to release the opening, and I tumbled in free fall through space. Except not dead. I could see into all the other pods, though, and in each one I could see Andrew's dead body, looking just like it did in the hospital after the crash.

Oh my God.

I'm going to throw up.

Saturday morning, after breakfast.

I made it to the bathroom before puking that time, so that's an improvement. Again, Selby was perfectly tranquil about it. He waited until I came back, helped me drink some water to clean my mouth, and then just sat there next to the bed, feet up on another chair, completely quiet.

I don't know how, but having him there helped calm me enough that I eventually drifted back to sleep.

I wanted to thank him for that this morning, but I'm starting to feel weird about all the thanking I'm doing. And, after all, he is technically my doctor right now, so he sort of has to do these things.

Mostly, I guess, I just want to thank him for letting me be me. But that's not the sort of thing you can tell a complete stranger "thank you" for.

Meeting Dr. Eggleston in just a few minutes. Hope he's not as bad as I'm expecting. Still feeling shaky from last night.

I thought I was done with nightmares. They finally stopped about three months ago, and I was really encouraged. I thought it was a sign that I was moving forward with healing, that things were getting better. That was about the same time that each day stopped being worse than the last, and started being either the same or a tiny bit easier. I was getting there.

And I know this is a huge upset, and anyone would be freaking out over what's happened to me, and so it's natural to have bad dreams. I just ... I could even handle the nightmares of being back in the pod, because that'd be normal, if terrifying. It's that the *dead Andrew* nightmares have come back that makes me want to give up.

I don't even have his picture with me. I sleep with my phone on the coffee table, not in my hand, so it didn't come with me like this journal did. At home, when I would wake up from a nightmare, I could turn on my phone and immediately see the last picture of him before the accident, and then I could close my eyes and hold that image in my head when I fell back asleep. I don't have that here. The only Andrew-image I have is the nightmare dead-Andrew.

It makes me sick just writing about it.

The Doc is scowling at me again. I've got to calm down or he's going to ban this journal for good.

My flaxen boy with laughing eyes
The sun played across your face
You grinned and held out your hand
So we could waltz along the shore
First I made you hold the pose
I took the picture

You rolled your eyes when I was done
We laughed together
Then we danced

That's the first poem I've written in over a year.

Saturday, after lunch.

I can't begin to express what writing that poem did for me. It just—I was thinking about the picture, and the next thing I knew, the words were flowing out of me. It's not the best poem I've ever written, not even close (it might even be pretty bad, but I'm refusing to edit or look at it too closely), but oh man. I suddenly feel a whole lot closer to *Riss*, to a person I was beginning to think had died along with Andrew.

It was good that I had that boost going into the meeting with Dr. Egghead, because he was a complete and total jerk, and if I'd still been shaky and distraught over my nightmare, he probably would have shredded me. As it was ...

Hold on, something is happening.

Senior staff meeting in sickbay, with yours truly as the topic and guest of honor! This should be interesting. Hope they don't mind sitting on hospital beds and drinking hay tea for the meeting.

(Everyone just came in and we're all sitting around, and I asked very politely if they minded me taking my own notes, and Captain Miles looked like he bit into a lemon but didn't refuse, so I'm very professionally writing this as it happens in the shorthand I learned in that college class my advisor told me was useless, and will fill it out longhand after. Captain Miles handed me a translator—very tiny, and fits inside my ear kind of like a hearing aid from my day—and told me I had to return it after the meeting, but since I had a legitimate concern in this matter, I needed to understand everything that was said. Captain Miles may have all the warmth of an Arctic icecap, but he makes it hard for me to hate him.)

Miles: We have the information from Earth. (*Turns and scowls at Riss.*)

Riss: Oh? (*Wondering why that's made him angrier at her.*)

Miles: And according to the reports, a Nerissa Waldon did, in fact, sign up for the bio-freeze.

Riss: Well, someone screwed up. I hope they fired him.

Chief Tyler: *laughs*

[*Side note: I know he's completely silver and shimmery and not-human, but holy cow, Tyler's smokin' hot. Bet all the single girls aboard the ship swoon for him.*]

Miles: You are entirely certain that you did not agree to participate in this?

Riss: Uh, yeah, that's not the sort of thing I would forget. (*Fairly certain he's obliquely accusing her of lying, but determined to rise above such petty accusations. Also, frankly, enjoying watching his face turn red as he gets more pissed.*)

Sapphira: Even if she did sign up, that doesn't explain why she survived when no one else did. Or why the project vanished so completely at the time. Or how she came out of deep freeze by herself, just in time for us to rescue her. Or, in fact, any of this at all.

Tyler: *applauds*

Sapphira, dryly: Thank you, Chief.

Tyler: *shuts up*

Dr Egghead: I find this young woman's tale entirely improbable, and frankly, think we need to apply Occam's Razor to the matter. What is the simplest explanation? That someone, aware of the failed bio-freeze affair, set it up to look like we'd found it, including a live body, which we would pull on board and would then insinuate herself amongst the crew. In short, officers, I believe she is an enemy spy.

Tyler: *snickers*

Selby: Are you insane, Eggleston?

Sapphira: That's certainly an interesting theory, Dr. Eggleston. But I'm not sure—

Tyler: Anyone who thinks that's the simplest explanation has got the most tortuous mind I've ever encountered. And that's saying something, when you consider my people.

Ru El: Does the Alliance have active enemies? Or do you believe this is a personal attack against you, Doctor, masterminded by a jealous rival? In which case, how would they get the resources? And how would they plant her this far out in space, where we are supposed to be the first Alliance ship ever to come?

Sapphira: Excellent points, Lieutenant, thank you.

Miles: Ms. Waldon, would you care to answer the doctor's charge?

Riss: Would it do me any good? If I were a spy, obviously I would deny it. Since I'm not, I *have* to deny it. Either way, I say 'no,' and either way, the good doctor's not going to believe me. He made that very clear when we met earlier.

Egghead: Her tales of Earth 500 years ago are utter nonsense.

Riss: Your history books suck.

Tyler, sotto voce: Every school child in the Alliance agrees with you.

Ru El: I would tend to believe the firsthand observer before the books written hundreds of years after the fact, personally.

Christensen: But we should take into account the possibility she is a spy, at least. (*Glances apologetically at Riss.*) I don't think she is. But we can't assume she isn't just because she seems like a nice person. Which you do. (*Reassuringly, to Riss, who somehow does not feel reassured.*)

Selby: There's something else you should take into account before you put Nerissa in front of the firing squad. Her DNA's wrong.

Long silence.

Miles: What?

Egghead: What?

Riss: *silent*

Selby: I've run every test I can think of. I've checked it over and over again. Her DNA is human, sure enough, but it's just ... off. (*Tosses Riss' personal, private medical reports onto the table for anyone and everyone to read.*)

Egghead: ...

Miles: ...

Et cetera from the rest of the crew.

Selby: See what I mean?
Egghead: This is impossible!
Selby: And yet, there it is.
Sapphira: But what does it mean?
Selby: I haven't got a clue.
Miles: I think we need to contact Earth again. Meeting adjourned.

Everyone leaves. Tyler turns and winks at Riss before he goes, and despite recognizing the signs of a chronic flirt with more charm than is good for him or anyone else, her spirits lift a little. And then sink again as the door to sickbay hisses closed, leaving her alone with a few nurses and Dr. What Hippocratic Oath? Selby.

I just finished transcribing my notes into longhand, having managed to successfully ignore Dr. Selby this entire time. I am so furious I could spit. Pretending to be all nice, and comforting, and friendly, while hiding my own medical facts from me, and then just announcing something like that to everyone including that jerk Egghead, and showing my records like they're public information. For all I know, they *are* public information, out there on this century's version of the internet!

He's side-eyeing me again. I don't even care. Let him try to take the journal away. Let him try to tell me what to do. You can't betray a person's privacy and then expect her to docilely accept whatever you tell her to do.

No one would *ever* have done that to Andrew. Nor to Roz or Mira, for that matter. I am so tired of being treated as less than a person.

This dragon
May be small
But her fire
Burns hot.

(Chorus for a new song, maybe?)

* * *

Saturday night.

I was all keyed up to roar at Dr. Selby when he came to take the pen away and tell me I'd been writing too much. Unfortunately, more pieces of the puzzle fell into place just then, so instead of giving him a lecture about breaches of privacy, I blurted out,

"Parallel universes!"

Whatever else he may be, the Doc isn't stupid. He stared at me open-mouthed for two seconds, then smacked his own forehead and said,

"Of course!"

He called Captain Miles (they have this ship's intercom-thing that can be set to either public, for "Now hear this, all hands ..." announcements, or private, like a regular phone call) and while they talked, I sat and thought about my genius realization.

It wasn't all my sci-fi interests that made it come together, weirdly enough. It was that Diana Wynne Jones series I'd loved as a kid, about the enchanter with nine lives and all the overlapping worlds, and when one person tried to skip into another world, it dragged her doppelgängers along behind her, each one spilling into the next world over. I was half tempted to stand up and shout "Chrestomanci" three times, just to see what would happen.

(Most likely a padded cell and straightjacket, so I didn't try.)

Talk about Occam's Razor! This is a way simpler explanation than me being a spy. The reason that this world's history had a record of Nerissa Waldon signing up for the bio-freeze while I didn't is because *she* was not *me*. Only somehow I got pulled in here instead. So was she in my world? And had she ended up in my future, or did she wake up on my couch Thursday, April 23, 2016, wondering what on earth had happened? Or had she ended up in yet another parallel world, with yet another Nerissa Waldon taking my place, an infinite number of Nerissas all skipping into the next world?

OK, not *perfectly* simple, but still better than the spy idea. This theory doesn't answer all our questions, but it makes so much sense, and was really quite proud of it when Sapphira and a minor scientist came around to better thrash it out (Captain Miles being too busy running the ship to come give this his personal attention and Dr.

Egghead refusing to come near me again).

The first thing Sapphira said was, "We have got to get you your own quarters."

I brightened up at that. Not only do I hate hospitals (sickbays, whatever. Potato, potahto), I was annoyed enough at Dr. Selby to want to get away from him, too. "Really?"

"She's still under medical observation," Dr. Selby said firmly. He wasn't officially part of the discussion, but was hovering near my bed anyway.

I was hugely tempted to stick my tongue out at him, but reminded myself that I am thirty years old, not twelve.

Sapphira kept looking all around, at the blank white walls and racks and trays of medical instruments, the medical staff wandering around, and the complete lack of privacy around my narrow bed and one small table. "She might get better faster if she were out of here, Doc."

"You insulting my sickbay?" he asked.

She shrugged. "Just an observation. No need to make it personal."

"You insulting my sickbay is personal, Commander."

"Ahem!" I said. "Not to be all 'me, me, me,' but hey. Could we talk about me just a little here, get that out of the way, and then you two can go back to bickering to your hearts' content?"

Selby grinned at me, but I refused to soften toward him.

"Right," Sapphira said, commandeering the Doc's gliding chair and spinning it around so she could sit in it backward, resting her hands on the top of its back, and her chin atop her hands. "Parallel worlds. It's a good thought, Nerissa. Really good. I'm hugely impressed."

"Absolutely," said the scientist, a slender, dark-skinned human (or at least he looks human) man around my age who'd introduced himself as Mark Danvers. "We should have thought of it ourselves."

"So those are an actual thing, not just a made-up notion for sci-fi?" I clarified.

"It's not been actually proven, and some scientists think it's nonsense, but there's enough evidence for it that I'm convinced, anyway," Danvers said.

"Besides, I've never, in my entire medical career, come across human DNA that looks like yours," Selby added. "The only explanation that makes sense is that you come from a universe that is almost, but not quite, a match of this one."

"Captain Miles wants you to keep testing her, each day, and checking the new results against the old," Sapphira said to him.

"Oh good," I interjected.

She raised one shoulder in a helpless shrug. "I know it's miserable for you, but we've never had a visitor from a parallel world here before that we know of. He wants to know if your DNA stays the same, or if it will start to adapt to our universe the longer you're here."

"That doesn't make any medical sense," Dr. Selby said.

Sapphira, Danvers, and I gave him equal stares, eyebrows raised and pursed lips.

"Fine, none of this makes sense," he conceded.

I didn't like that the Captain got to order tests on me without asking my consent, any more than I liked Selby revealing my private medical details without my consent, but this didn't seem like the time to bring it up. "So do we have a theory about how and why I'm here?"

"We're working on it," Danvers said.

Sapphira cleared her throat. "Along those lines, I'm afraid I need to ask you for some details about your life—we need to compare your experiences with what history tells us about our Nerissa Waldon, so we can get some idea of where the lives merge and where they are the same, and how and why you crossed over."

The sympathetic look on her face was enough to tell me that she'd already learned plenty about this Nerissa, and that Andrew had most likely died in this universe as well (well, why else would she sign up for the bio-freeze?).

I hated that I had to talk about it to people I barely knew, but at least Sapphira asked, instead of ordering. "All right," I said, fingers fiddling restlessly with the blanket's edge. "Look, I know I'm under medical observation, but could we possibly go somewhere else to talk about this? Even just a walk around the ship?"

Dr. Selby looked like he wanted to object, but Sapphira stood up and simply dominated the entire room, filling it with this aura of her authority. I so want to learn how to do that, but I suppose her years in the AEF have something to do with it. "Absolutely," she said. "I take full responsibility for this, Doctor," she added.

He snapped his mouth closed and nodded.

"No more than twenty minutes," he said. "And no damned journal writing afterward!"

Danvers had the good sense to stay behind, and Sapphira and I walked around the corridors. If I hadn't been so focused on keeping my emotions under control, I'm pretty sure I would have been fascinated by the ship. It's not huge, as ships go in the AEF (so Sapphira says). Crew complement of about forty, not including the dozen scientists on board. But it's fast, and it's maneuverable, and much better equipped for a long-term deep space mission like this than the bigger ships.

So we paced steadily through some of the more deserted areas, and I kept my eyes fastened on the floor (metal, and covered in some sort of springy coating that felt cool and firm-but-not-painful to my bare feet) and told her the bare details of my life. Two sisters, two parents, all still alive, handful of aunts and uncles and cousins, one deceased husband, a few friends. Double major in English and Music in college. Assistant manager of the local second-hand bookshop, and had independently produced one CD (I had to explain to her what a CD was) and was working on a second when husband's car accident happened.

She nodded and kept looking at her handheld device, which looked like a fancy e-reader to me. "Everything matches up," she said. "I'm not getting any clues."

It helped, a lot, that she was so professional about it. No sympathy, no "Oh Riss, you poor little thing," just cool comparison between my story and other-Nerissa's.

She dropped me back off to sickbay, and Dr. Selby fussed until he had ascertained that I was undamaged from my dangerous peregrinations. I pacified him by resting for a few hours, and since I was a good little girl, he agreed that I could write in my journal until supper.

Saturday, Later.

* * *

Really, really nice.

Chief Tyler dropped by at suppertime with a tray of his own and asked if I minded some company with my meal. It's quite possible he did so out of pity, but he didn't actually act pitying, so I don't mind even if his motivation was something less than a desire to get to know me.

Besides, he is just as fun as I suspected. Outrageously flirtatious, but in such a way that it's impossible to take him seriously.

I asked him about his planet and people. He's from the planet *A'nah'merah'leshanaharah*, which most other peoples shorten to "Anah," and they were the next planet to join the Alliance after Koloth. Curiously, Tyler's people are only one of five sentient species on Anah, all of whom are now part of the Alliance. *Fascinating*.

Then Tyler wanted to know what it was about my report of life on Earth 500 years ago that bothered Dr. Eggleston so much, and I told him it was mostly that we weren't as barbaric as he seemed to believe.

"That must have been a disappointment to him," he agreed gravely.

Then I asked about what life was like in the AEF, and he regaled me with stories of his time in the Fleet—his people are long-lived, so even though he's the equivalent of a human in his thirties, he's actually much older. We talked about some of the planets he's visited and sights he's seen, and I did my best to not drool over how fascinating it all sounded, until Selby kicked him out and said I needed to get some sleep.

I'm not as worried about nightmares tonight. I've been thinking about Andrew and not talking about him, holding him as tight to me as I could, ever since waking up in the coffin, and I think telling Sapphira about him, without getting all emotional about it, helped me step back and regain my equilibrium. If I had to guess, I'd suspect that I'll probably have claustrophobia nightmares again, but hopefully no more dead-husband dreams.

Please, God.

Sunday, April 26, 2016/Day Four of my Wild Space Adventure.

I awoke this morning from a sleep plagued by no nightmares at all. I stretched luxuriously, amazed anew at what a difference a good night's sleep makes to one's general sense of well-being. The previous day I'd been groggy and dull, letting Dr. Selby and Captain Miles and Dr. Eggleston yank me around and make decisions for me and accuse me of being a liar.

Ah, who am I fooling. It wasn't the lack of sleep. It was me again, just me. Doing what I've always done, retreating in the face of other people's confidence, believing in their superiority until they start to believe it too.

Roz and Mira were seemingly born with the innate knowledge that they deserve love and respect simply by virtue of being alive. Not me. Growing up, everything I did, said, and thought had to be justified, if not to other people than at least to me. I felt—at least until I met Andrew—that I had to earn every ounce of affection, every crumb of respect, from others and from myself.

No one ever said this outright, or ever treated me badly, but the beliefs of all three of us were so ingrained in us and in our parents, grandparents, etc., that we all acted that way without even realizing it.

It took Andrew, a complete outsider, someone who hadn't grown up with all of us, to see the damage that was being done. Even then, it was only after years of his gentle encouragement and support that I was able to see it for myself.

Roz and Mira couldn't understand why 'little Rissy" started withdrawing from them, no longer letting them dictate my every move simply by making me feel stupid and guilty for doing anything but what they wanted. They only knew that it had happened after I got involved with Andrew, and they blamed him for "turning me against the family."

Tensions were high ever since Andrew and I married, and the way my sisters tried to reel me back in after Andrew's death only made things worse.

I've got goosebumps on my arms as I relive all these memories. Selby, Captain Miles, and Dr. Eggleston aren't my sisters, but without an Andrew here to give me strength, I'm not sure who I am. Even the memories of him, so sustaining in the home we had shared and the life we had built together, seem faded and distant here.

Distant to the tune of 500 years and goodness only knows how many millions of miles.

Time to take a break from these depressing thoughts to get dressed and ready for the day. Whatever "the day" brings. Dr. Selby is nowhere to be seen this morning, his junior medical officer is in charge for a change. I'm not sure why Selby decided to take a break from sickbay, other than that even the most dedicated doctor needs to go off duty once in a while, but I'm cravenly glad to put off a confrontation with him.

He'd been *nice* to me—no, not nice. Anyone could be nice. It doesn't mean a thing. This is worse. He'd been kind to me, and that's going to make it all the harder to stand up against him and force him to treat me with respect. Just *thinking* about it makes me sick to my stomach.

I emerged from the bathroom (head, Sapphira calls it) after getting dressed and cleaning my teeth to find Tyler waiting for me.

"Nerissa Waldon, just the person I wanted to see!" he cried, straightening up from a graceful lounge against the half-wall separating Selby's office from the rest of sickbay.

"Why?" I asked suspiciously.

He laughed and draped an arm around my shoulders, guiding me to the big window opening up to the blackness of space and the brightness of stars. "See out there?" he said, waving with his free hand. "See all that? We're part of that, Nerissa, one piece of all that beauty."

"Oo-kay," I said, wondering if this had a point.

"One of those shining points out there is a planet on which we will land in just three days. So far as we know, it is uninhabited by sentient beings, just ready and waiting for us to explore. I want *you*, Nerissa Waldon, to be one of those people." He stepped back and beamed at me.

I gaped. "Me?" I said ungrammatically.

"Oh Tyler," said Sapphira, having entered unnoticed by either of us. "The Captain'll never go for that."

Tyler raised silver hand. "Ah, but the Captain is not in charge of the landing team, is he, dear Commander? You are."

I bit my lip, trying not to look too much like a puppy begging for a treat but expecting a kick instead.

"Give me one good reason why I should take someone with no training or experience on a landing party to a potentially dangerous planet," Sapphira said, her eyes sweeping my face and then returning to Tyler's.

"Exactly," he said, as though she had made his point for him. "She's never done anything like this before, and if we manage to get her back to her proper place and time, she never will again. Have a heart, Commander. Give the lady a proper adventure. You don't want her to go back to her old life saying 'Well, that was a lovely sickbay and nothing else I experienced on my space adventure,' do you?"

Sapphira paused. I held my breath. Tyler looked over at me and winked. Finally, Sapphira burst into her rich, rolling laugh.

"I swear, your tongue is as golden as your eyes," she said.

Tyler stuck that member out. "Nope," he said around it. "Brown." (I tried not to stare.)

Sapphira ignored this and turned to me. "Do you want to come? Honest answer, don't be swayed by this madman here."

"Yes," I said, not letting myself think too much about it. "That is, as long as you don't think I'd be in the way or a nuisance or anything."

Sapphira tapped a finger on her cheek, considering. "All right," she said. "As long as the Doc clears it, and as long as you can figure out the patois enough that we won't have to worry if the translators don't work on the surface, you can come. Tyler's right. You should have some fun while you're stuck here."

"Thanks," I said, feeling rather like beaming myself.

"Tyler, Captain Miles's looking for you," Sapphira said, nodding and dismissing the matter. "Has a question about the port engine."

Tyler sighed and raised his hands toward the ceiling. "Alas, an engineer's work is never done!"

"You'd better hope not, or you'd become obsolete," Sapphira said, and with a quick goodbye, the two left the sickbay, leaving me alone, aside from the medical crew.

You'd better believe I'm going to study up on the patois now. A chance to explore an alien world? *So cool*. And if Selby tries to tell me I can't go, I'll ...

Honestly, I'll probably wither and do nothing, but I'll at least try to defy him.

Sunday, Later.

Begged a hand reader off Sapphira and she downloaded some history documents onto it for me, so I spent the rest of the day reading up on what happened on Earth—this Earth—in the last 500 years. As Tyler said, I don't want to return to my own place and time without having a clue about anything outside the walls of this sickbay.

I confess to usually thinking history's fairly dry stuff (unless music is involved), but since this is *future* history for me, I didn't have any problems engaging. This is where my world is heading! I'll get to be all smug when (if) I get back and people start talking about where the human race will be in a few hundred years, because *I will know*. Even if I can't tell anyone.

As best I can tell, the discovery of Arethra and start of the Alliance marked a slow transition from a Renaissance-type Era into a new Industrial Era, which explains why clothing and other design is so graceful and pretty, and yet people's attitudes definitely tend more toward practical and functional. I saw an illustration of some Earth city-forests, where trees have grown up and homes have been built in and around them, and they are connected by road-type tracks in the branches, everything above the ground, and it's so beautiful it makes my heart ache to have that right now—in my now—to live in a place that harmonizes with nature so much.

At the same time, they are building ships for exploration and protection, and creating new tech all the time—nanotechnology is pretty big right now, feeding a design into a computer and letting the nanos create it—and really moving away from beauty being valued in and of itself in favor of only useful things having value.

This is all big-picture stuff, of course. I still don't have much idea of what day-to-day life looks like for the average citizen on Earth. What jobs are like and how people spend their time, and what they do for entertainment, and oh, little things. How does one go grocery shopping now? What's the internet like? Why hasn't anyone invented site-to-site transporters yet? How does it work to still have independent countries all around Earth, and yet have there be one centralized government over it all?

Gosh, if they can't get me back, I suppose I could spend the next eight years doing nothing more than studying so as to be prepared for life back on Earth. Ghastly thought, though. I've never exactly been drawn to a scholarly life.

Monday, April 27, 2016/Day 5 of life aboard the Caledonia.

Thank God, thank God. I had one nightmare of being trapped in a coffin again, but I woke myself from it with a kind of shuddering gasp, not a scream, and even though Selby (back on duty, naturally) came right over to check me, I didn't need any babying. He took my vitals, and I ignored his presence and rolled over to go back to sleep.

No Andrew at all. Thank God.

It occurred to me this morning in the shower that I was being completely stupid about this privacy and control thing. Here I am, in a brand-new universe. Nobody knows me at all. I can be anyone I want. I don't have to be tiny little Rissy, babied and coddled and smothered by her loving family and kindly condescended to by everyone else. I can be the person I was with Andrew, even if he's not here. This is my chance to stop being small.

The dragon's wings begin to grow
It still takes courage to make them go.

I marched out of the shower in my latest set of borrowed finery (a deep green wide-collared tunic with asymmetrical hem and black velvety-soft leggings) and walked right up to where Selby was sitting at his desk.

"You should have told me about my DNA before you announced it to the entire senior staff," I said without any "good morning" or anything. He dropped his hand reader and looked at me like I'd grown a second head, a considerably bolder and mouthier one. "And you should have asked for my permission before sharing my medical report with everyone. I don't know what sort of code you doctors follow in this century, but that's just basic courtesy. Just because I'm from the past, and a different universe, doesn't mean that you can get away with treating me like I'm not a competent, sane person. And no more tests and blood-work unless I say so. I'm not going to say no if asked," I had to add, "but I still want to *be* asked."

He stood up and stared at me. I stared back, willing my hands to stop trembling and shrieking silently at myself to not back down.

"You're right," he finally said, sitting back down. "I started thinking of you as a test subject instead of a person. That was completely wrong. I'm sorry."

And that was that.

It almost felt anticlimactic, but it also felt wonderful, that he treated my personal Declaration of Independence so matter-of-factly instead of arguing with me and insisting that he knew better than me and I should just trust him, and "Stop blowing this out of proportion and being so *dramatic* about everything, Rissy."

I'm starting to understand that I haven't been battling against other people's poor opinion so much my entire life as I have my own assumption that everyone *is going* to think poorly of me. That paranoia has been helped by my family's utter and complete refusal to look at me as a person, but maybe if I had stopped expecting that of them, they would have stopped treating me as "just" little Rissy.

You know what I think I like best about this universe? Nobody calls me Rissy.

No Sapphira, Tyler, or Danvers this morning. Instead, Lieutenant-Commander Natalie Christensen dropped in to see me.

"I thought I should get to know the person who keeps wearing my clothes," she said cheerfully.

I've enough cultural stereotypes ingrained in me to wonder how an Asian girl has a French first name and Swedish surname, and am aware enough of those stereotypes to be disgusted at my surprise. Jeez, get a life, Riss.

(Actually, any name criticism at all would be hysterically funny coming from me, considering I and my sisters are named Rosalind, Nerissa, and Miranda. Much as I love Shakespeare, before I'd inflict those names on helpless children …!)

She promptly told me to call her Chris, and I surprised myself by telling her I usually go by Riss.

"It's a freakin' comedy act," Dr. Selby muttered when we started laughing about the rhyme, by which I deduced that I must be doing enough better for him to stop being nice to me.

He has a point. "Chris and Riss" does sound like a bad comic duo.

Chris and I are about the same size (small), which is why her clothes fit me so well, but she is fantastically fit, really lithe and toned, while one solid year of grief has left me squishy and slumped. Not that life as a bookseller/musician lends itself to physical fitness anyway. She wears her black hair long and loose, except for two bright red fishtail braids going back just above her ears. She looks kind of like a petite Lord of the Rings elf with awesome fashion sense.

Chris is Chief of Security, a hugely important posting, and it's her first mission as such, and underneath her boundless enthusiasm I can tell she's scared to death she'll screw this up. It is a lot of responsibility, and she's only twenty-three. Getting posted to this ship was a huge, huge honor, especially for someone as young as she is, and as new to this role. Apparently Captain Miles specifically requested her, which is another point in his favor, darn it. I don't *want* to think well of him.

Chris asked Dr. Selby for permission to show me some more of the ship. I guess everyone but Dr. Egghead has rejected the "maybe Riss is a spy" theory, and so Captain Miles gave permission for me to see some of the non-vital parts. Not the bridge, duh, and not Engineering or a couple other places, but everything else.

Selby agreed, and added, "Another night like the last two nights and we can think about finding you some quarters of your own. I might even agree to Tyler's insane idea of letting you join his landing party."

I beamed at him as I left sickbay, and my last sight of him was him blinking his eyes and looking a bit stunned. I suppose I really haven't looked that happy since arriving.

The fact that it was my screaming night horror keeping me in sickbay is slightly mortifying. It also confirms my belief that Dr. Selby is quite sweet underneath his crankiness. He didn't—doesn't—want me to have to endure that alone, nothing medical about it.

Chris had a great time showing off the ship. My favorite place is the mess, where the crew tends to hang out when not on duty. The food's not so great, but the atmosphere is swell (there's an advertising slogan for you). Everyone is really stoked to be on this mission, even after two years away from home, and they're all so proud of what they're doing, and excited by what they've already found and will continue to find. I might have to revise my opinion of them all as selfish idiots for coming on this voluntarily, even the married ones.

The AEF uniforms are brown and cream, very natty and sharp. Brown leggings with a stripe down the outside, different color stripes representing different honors—crimson being the highest possible, cream being the basic "yay you made it aboard a ship" stripe everyone starts out with. Cream long-sleeved, form-fitting tunic with a scoop neck and asymmetric hem. Cropped brown jacket with cream trim. Some of them have a brown vest instead of jacket, which looks much more casual and I guess is the relaxed version of the uniform. Dark brown wide belt to hold weapons, tools, etc. Soft ankle boots for on board the ship, hard knee-high boots for landing parties.

The scientists have their own variation of the uniform, same style but crimson and navy instead of cream and brown, and the off-duty crew members almost always wear brown wide-legged pants and the cream tunics. Chris is one of the few who actually likes to wear civilian clothes whenever she gets a chance.

"Some people look at it almost as a slur to the Fleet, if you don't wear either the uniform or the off-duty version all the time except on leave," she said. "As proud as I am of being part of it, though, I love clothes too much to give them all up." And she laughed.

There's also some sort of ranking protocol involved. Ensigns and non-commissioned crew are not allowed to wear civilian clothes except on leave, and only commanders and above get to be creative with their uniform, like Sapphira, who wears her vest with a sleeveless top underneath.

I asked Chris when I'd be able to get some clothes of my own and stop raiding her closet, and she said she didn't know, and took me to the Logistics Specialist. She (LS Petty Officer Parminetra, of the Roctan people, from one of the moons orbiting Anah— she is roughly humanoid in shape, covered in reddish-brown fur, with fangs instead of teeth) told me that the only extra clothing they have in stock are uniform pieces, and I'm not eligible to wear them. Dire Things, apparently, will happen to a civilian who wears AEF clothing, even the off-duty outfit. Running around naked would be a better option.

So I'm stuck with sharing Chris' clothes for now, unless someone else of a similar size and species decides to donate something to the cause. We can't exactly order something from Earth and have it shipped to us, after all, and replicators (Digital Transformers, or DTs) take up way too much energy to be useful aboard a ship, so nothing doing there.

"So no making something out of nothing?" I asked half-heartedly, and Chris and PO Parminetra both laughed. I'd already put Chris in stitches earlier by asking in all seriousness about transporters. She thinks it hugely funny how much of what they take for granted is mind-blowing to me (like aliens), and then the other things that I think they must have developed by now she says are scientifically impossible.

I get the impression Chris thinks I'm hugely funny in general. I don't mind. She reminds me of an overgrown puppy, and I have to stop myself from patting her on the head and telling her what a good girl she is, yes she is, who's a good girl then.

Back to clothes. Chris doesn't mind sharing for now, and she says that maybe one of the planets we explore will have a market where we can look for some new stuff for me. She told me about this one place that sold this amazing silk-type fabric, all sleek and smooth and looking like sunlight moving across water, and she was able to find a tailor there who made it into this stunning dress for her, and then she dragged me off to her quarters to show it to me (holy cow, that's all I can say about that. Why couldn't I have arrived here before they reached *that* place?). Then back to the mess where she and some of her pals told me more stories about the different places they've been, and I would have suspected them of pulling my leg if they hadn't been so transparently thrilled with it all.

Then we had lunch, and now I'm back in sickbay resting, studying up on the patois, and feeling very, very old for being so exhausted after spending only a few hours with that sort of enthusiasm.

Heh. I mentioned that last bit to Dr. Selby, who replied that even Chris gets worn out by her own enthusiasm, and not to worry about it.

Monday, later.

Thinking about friends in general today. I think I'm starting to believe I'll never get back to my own time and space, and I'm weirdly un-freaked by it. I don't care to analyze that too much just yet. It's making me think about my friends, and how you just always assume they'll be there until they're gone. I think those of us in our closest circle stopped taking each other for granted after Andrew's death, but I certainly never imagined a reality where they'd still be alive, and I'd still be alive, and yet we'd never see or talk to each other again.

OK. Technically, I know that, if I'm 500 years in the future, they aren't alive anymore. But this parallel universe thing makes it seem more like ... I don't know, more like our two timelines are running alongside each other, just out of sync, and my friends and life are still ticking along at the same pace as this life here, just out of my reach. That might not be scientifically accurate, but that's how it feels.

There's Megan and Tom, who were our closest friends before, and my rocks after, the accident. I can't imagine never sitting in their kitchen with the kids running around madly and Tom shouting about something-or-other from the study, while Megan ignores the chaos and tranquilly sips her tea and listens to my latest song.

Then there's Sarah, my fellow creative-buddy, whose medium is painting and drawing instead of music and poetry. She's the one who talked me into my nose ring (Andrew howled with laughter for days after we got it done—I hadn't told him about it beforehand—I walked into the apartment with it and he just choked. He came around eventually, and finally confessed that he thought it was sexy), and just in the last month she'd been trying to convince me to cut my hair and dye it purple. I think it was her way of urging me toward *living* again, instead of just existing.

I almost did it, too

Andrew's best friend Mike, who went into a mourning almost as deep as mine when Andrew died. He asked me to marry him six months ago, not because he loved me, but because he felt it was his responsibility to take care of me now that Andrew was gone. It was sweet, and I told him so, but I still refused. We wouldn't have been compatible at all. He accepted that, and told me if I ever changed my mind, just to let him know.

I hope he finds himself a nice girl someday.

Then there are the ladies from my wine-and-book club, not as close as the others but they still rallied round and lent me their strength when I had none left of my own. The folks at church, who brought meals and prayed sincerely and never once piously told me that Andrew's death was God's will. They helped me when I felt God had abandoned me, were never Job's comforters. I am so deeply thankful for all of them.

I'm glad to have gotten to know Chris a little. It makes me feel a little less uprooted, feeling like I've taken the first steps toward making a friend. Not that Sapphira and Tyler —and Dr. Selby too, a little—haven't been friend-ish, but not quite the same. For all of them I tend to feel more like part of their duty. Chris, though, seemed to genuinely want to hang out with me, to want to get to know me just for me. Chatting with her about clothes and daily ship life felt blessedly normal.

I wonder how she feels about purple hair?

Tuesday, April 28, 2016/Day 6 aboard the Caledonia.

Chris and Sapphira both think purple hair would be a great look on me. Dyeing is apparently really easy now, so even on an AEF ship like this one they could help. Now we're trying to figure out if there's a short cut they could give me that wouldn't make my hair poof around my head like a mushroom. Dr. Selby looks more and more disgusted at our girly conversation with each passing moment. I think he's going to be as glad to get me out of sickbay as I am to go.

Because—yes! Only a brief nightmare about drowning, of all things, last night, and no screaming or puking, so he's cleared me to leave *and* to join tomorrow's landing party on the unknown planet. I still need to come back every morning before breakfast for more bloodwork, but other than that, my time is now my own. I agreed, and we were both very formal and polite about it, and for the first time I saw a hint of respect, as well as the usual sympathy and crankiness, in his eyes.

Captain Miles-to-go-before-I-sleep, so I understand, is Not Happy about assigning me to crew quarters, but it's either that or stick me in with the scientists, and Dr. Egghead threw a major hissy fit over the thought of having me anywhere near "his" people, so I get a tiny little cabin toward the nose (front? Prow? Bow?), which is apparently the least desirable part of the ship, don't ask me why.

I asked how there happened to be empty cabins at all, and Sapphira and Chris, who both came to help me move, glanced at each other, before Sapphira explained in an unusually gentle tone that they've lost a few crew members since starting out.

So I am sleeping in a dead person's cabin.

This didn't bother me as much as they clearly assumed it was going to. I figured it had to be something like that. As long as I don't know too much about the person who held it before me, I think I'll be fine.

Moving out of sickbay isn't going to take long. My tiny pile of Chris-clothes, this journal and pen, my pajamas (thankfully now clean), my underwear tube, and that's it.

Tuesday, later.

* * *

I am writing this from my own quarters, with no scowling doctor commenting loudly to the room at large that "Silence is golden" applies to writing *or* speaking, and he cannot imagine how my poor head must feel, to be crammed with so many thoughts that require *this much* writing down.

Ha. If only you knew, Dr. Selby, that this journal doesn't even hold the half of what I'm going through.

Because really, it doesn't. The internal freak-outs, the fuming, the moments of utter panic where I cannot breathe because of the reality of the situation, the emotions too big for words ... I haven't been writing those down. How could I?

I miss my guitar. I think I'd write less if I could play more. I even miss piano, which is saying something. Heck, I'd pick up a fiddle and mess around with it if I had the chance, which I haven't willingly done since college.

Sapphira and Chris got me settled, with my Chris-clothes in the tiny closet and my journal on the equally tiny desk, and then we three had glorious fun figuring out what to do with the rest of the place.

Here is my cabin: the door vanishes with a hiss when I put my new personal code into the lock or invite someone in, then reappears when I tell it to close, or tap my code in a second time. Walking in, there is a door leading to my bathroom on the left, my bunk on the right, closet next to the bathroom, and the desk against the far wall. Next to the desk is a little round window, a porthole really, and a scooped-out nook right beneath where I can curl up and watch the stars.

I love it. Sapphira and Chris were both apologetic, and taken aback when I raved about it. Yes, it's tiny and sparse and it takes me about three steps to move from bed to bathroom, but it's all mine, and it's private, and it feels cozy and secure, and there's even a window so I don't get claustrophobic.

"You're so grateful for the simplest things, Riss," Sapphira said with a puzzled-eyebrows look at me.

Maybe I am, but they don't seem that simple to me. Coming from a family where everything I was and did was taken for granted, where anything I asked for was treated as an enormous burden or hugely ridiculous, to have people show concern for even the little details—like Dr. Selby getting me a comb, like Sapphira remembering my claustrophobia and making sure I have a window in my cabin—is wonderful and refreshing.

They set me up with my own computer and hand reader, both old, junky ones according to their standards, but whoa, way cool for this cavewoman. This century's version of the Internet is amazing. And, score, tons of books from my day (from my day—I sound like an old biddy. You kids get off my lawn!) are now public domain, so I can download them all for free. Which is really great, since I have no money and I refuse to pirate anything, and there's no ship's library.

Sapphira showed me how to download projections to appear on my walls like pictures, and Chris helped me pick some out. Above my bunk, covering almost the entire wall, is this image of a forest, in Scotland I think, all green and mysterious and deep, with shadows and sun. It is so calming, and I know I'll be able to sleep better with having that there.

Between the closet and bathroom doors I have a small image of the *Caledonia*, which since I've never seen it from the outside is handy for reminding me what my new home looks like (long, pointed at the front and broad in the back like an awesome space dagger, shiny, and totally sci-fi, for the record. Very old-school design, according to Chris. Classic, according to Sapphira). Plus both Sapphira and Chris got these pleased expressions when I asked for it, so I'm glad I could make them happy.

I want a quote above my desk, but I haven't been able to choose one yet. The first book I downloaded was the Oxford Book of English Verse, and I'm going to read through it, a little each night after I finish journaling and before I fall asleep, until I've found the perfect quote to go with my new life.

Sapphira suggested "Keep Calm and Carry On," so I see *that* meme has survived another few hundred years. The power of the British Empire, God Save the Queen. Or whomever is ruling there now.

After that, we looked up pictures of hair, and found one that we all decided would work, and they called for Chris's friend Ona to come over. She came in and cut and dyed my hair, and now I have these shiny purple ringlets all over my head. It looks fabulous. Ona's a genius with hair. She blushed like mad when I told her that, and hurried away again.

Sarah would be so proud. Andrew would fall over if he could see me now, but then he'd come around and decide he loves it because I do.

After lunch, Sapphira and Chris had to get back to their real duties, not their Riss-duties, so I hung out in my cabin by myself and reveled in the silence while looking up information like mad. 500 years of culture and history to catch up on, a new-ish language to master, and all I *really* want to do is check to see if my—or rather, other-Nerissa's—indie album is still out there.

Don't do it, Riss.

I also want to look up everything about Roz and Mira and Mom and Dad and everyone else, and Megan and Tom and Sarah and Mike—find out their lives, if they've still got descendants floating around, how long they lived, how many kids they named after me, all that.

Total, sheer, dangerous self-indulgence.

I keep reminding myself that what happens in this universe doesn't exactly match what happens in mine, and it doesn't matter so much what everyone did and how they lived here, and so looking them up won't really tell me anything about *my* people.

It's still tempting.

I finally shut it off and buried myself in a book. Kind of cheating, but awesome, to get the final book in my current favorite series a year before it publishes in my-time.

I skipped dinner, which I'm sure would annoy the Doc but I often do, it's not a big deal. Besides, I'm not entirely certain how to get to the mess from here, and I don't want to call Chris or Sapphira and ask.

Crap. Just realized that I also have no idea how to get back to sickbay from here. I don't think it's even on the same deck. Hopefully I'll run into a friendly crew member tomorrow morning who'll show me. And then draw me a map.

Going to read some poetry now and call it a night.

* * *

Later, possibly early tomorrow morning.

It figures that my first night on my own would give me screaming nightmares again.

I need to ask Chris how to get music on my computer. Would give anything to be able to listen to some old hymns right about now.

Going to write, and then read for a while instead. Hope I'll be able to get back to sleep at some point, or Selby will take one look at my haggard face and order me right back to sickbay.

Right after Andrew died, if I stopped for two seconds to realize what had happened, I would want to curl into a tiny ball and howl. So instead I just kept going and moving forward, hoping eventually it would stop being fake.

And slowly, it was getting there. I had moments—never more than that, but still, moments where I could pause and breathe, and be at peace. Where I could briefly acknowledge my loss and accept it, before the panic would crash back in on me and my brain would shut down again. Moments where I could laugh and genuinely feel joy.

Then this happened, and I'm right back to having to go, go, go, laugh and talk and move and be logical, because if I stop to breathe I will begin screaming and never stop.

When I'm asleep, the reality of it all comes crashing back in on me and reduces me to a gibbering mess.

I want to go home.

I want my husband.

I want my old life back.

But even if I go home, I can't have that. Home isn't home anymore, not really.

This ripping away from my world has brought into stark clarity a truth I've avoided for an entire year: that no matter how well I heal, no matter how normal I try to keep my life, no matter how well I adjust, *he's never coming back*. This isn't some sort of test or trial, where you have to endure for a time and then it gets better.

The life I loved ended the day of that car accident. I might, in time, gain a new life that I also love, but that old life's never coming back. I've been refusing to look at that for an entire year, because I couldn't handle it. Getting sent here is making it incredibly plain. I can't hide from the truth any longer.

No wonder I keep having nightmares.

Ugh. I'm getting maudlin. Time to find some more books.

Wednesday, April 29, 2016/Day 7.

I fell asleep at my desk last night and woke this morning to my wall squawking at me.

It took me a ridiculously long time to figure out what it was (my intercom), and then an even longer time to figure out how to work it (voice commands, and don't I feel stupid now for smacking it half a dozen times). Finally, I was able to answer, and of course it was Dr. Selby.

"Are you sick?" he demanded without even saying good morning.

"Ungh?" I answered because, like I said, I had just woken up. I cleared my throat and tried again. "No?"

"You're late," he said.

"Didn't realize we had a specific appointment," I said. "You said before breakfast. I haven't had breakfast yet. Therefore, I am not late."

"Don't get cute," he said.

"Aw, and you haven't even seen my hair yet," I replied, waking up more fully and surprising myself by enjoying teasing him.

His snort came through as a burst of static.

I laughed. "I overslept," I said. "Let me get showered and dressed and then I'll be right there."

"I wait with bated breath," he said, and hung up.

I realized a moment too late that I forgot to ask him how to get to sickbay.

I shrugged and stepped into my teensy-tiny bathroom (head! I must learn to use the proper terms for things and places here), and the shower that is barely big enough for me. I hope the last crew member to have this room was not a guy, or a girl as tall as Sapphira, or one of the taller alien species, because they would seriously have had to fold themselves in half to get clean.

On the other hand, at least every cabin gets its own shower and toilet. Showers are amazing here, water sprays at you from above and all four sides, and you can adjust how strong or soft you want it with a simple tap on the wall. The toilets are ... well, toilets. Self-cleaning, at least, which is *awesome*. Let's hear it for nanos, which are all throughout the ship constantly turning dirt and bad bacteria *et al* into good! *Everything* is recycled here, from water to waste.

I don't have any makeup with me, so I couldn't do anything to disguise the black circles under my eyes, but if I was lucky the purple curls would distract the Doc from my face.

I wore the purple top and blue leggings again, cleaned my teeth, and braved myself for the trip to sickbay. I stepped into the corridor and looked up and down hopefully.

Not one person in sight!

I at least remembered the basic direction we had come from yesterday, so I turned right and trotted off, trying to reconstruct our journey. We'd taken a few turns, but passed some other turns to go straight, and I couldn't remember which we had done where. And then there was the hoverlift, which operates like an elevator and makes it easy to get between decks, and I honestly had no idea if we'd taken it up or down.

I wandered around hopelessly for a while, not seeing anything that looked remotely familiar (or rather, it all looked far too familiar—everything looked exactly the same as everything else, nothing to make it stand out). Eventually I noticed numbers and letters painted at various junctions: 3Ba, 3Bf, 3C, that sort of thing. I brilliantly deduced this meant I was on the third deck, and that one could follow the letters to orient oneself on a map.

Since I had no map, nor any idea how many decks there were, or what deck sickbay was on, this did not leave me that much better off than I was before.

Finally, I saw Chief PO Tyler at a distant junction. He turned when I called his name, and grinned as though he was happier to see me than anyone else in two universes.

"Our intrepid traveler!" he said, walking toward me with his arms spread wide. "What can I do for you? Excited about the mission later today? Wandering the corridors in itchy anticipation of setting your feet on hopefully-firm ground again?"

"I am so lost," I confessed.

He laughed. His voice isn't as rich as Dr. Selby's, but his laugh is the kind that makes you feel all warm and snuggly inside. I grinned back at him.

"Where do you want to go?" he asked.

"Many, many places," I told him. "But right now I'm supposed to be in sickbay for more bloodwork."

"Ah, the thrilling life of a voyager between realities."

"Yes, I hear there's talk of a book deal."

He laughed again and draped one silver arm over my shoulder. "I think I'm going to like having you around, Nerissa. You don't mind if I call you Nerissa?"

"Riss, please," I said.

"Riss it is. All these Fleet people are so stuffy, bound by rules and regulations. And don't even get me started on the scientists. It's about time we had someone on board who knows how to enjoy life." He fluttered his eyelashes—which are long and curly and most women back home would die for—at me, and I laughed.

I don't like being flirted with seriously. I still wear my wedding ring, and if a guy genuinely hits on a woman who, to all appearances, is married, he's a creep and should be pushed into a lake. But Tyler—I know his type, even if the ones I know are human and he is not. He's one of those who can't help flirting, but who never means it. It's like there's so much charm inside of him that it has to escape somehow, and that's its only outlet.

People like that are just plain fun to be around, for me anyway.

He got me safely to sickbay and showed me how to tap the letters/numbers at any junction to bring a map of the ship springing to life in the air. Then all I have to do is say where I want to go, and it highlights the best path from here-to-there. Very cool. He even showed me how to operate the hoverlift (which they just call the "lift," how very British) so I don't need to freak out about that.

Then he told me I was welcome to come to Engineering any time.

"Captain Miles informed me Engineering was off-limits," I said.

"A girl can't help it if she gets lost wandering around a great big ship like this and accidentally ends up in an off-limits section, can she?"

(I am seriously tempted.)

By the time I actually got into sickbay Dr. Selby wanted to know just how long of a shower I'd taken.

"I would have been here sooner if someone had bothered to show me how to find my way around," I said.

He blinked. "Hm."

I felt a little bad about my criticism. After all, it wasn't like I had mentioned to him or anyone else that I was clueless about getting around the ship.

"Chief Tyler got me here," I added. "And in one piece, no less."

"Considering Tyler, that's pretty close to a miracle," Selby said.

"So why'd you oversleep?" he asked as I perched on the bed and held out my arm for him to draw the blood.

I should have known he wouldn't overlook that.

"Hard time sleeping last night," I said briefly.

"More nightmares?"

I bit back a sigh. He was my doctor. It was his job to pry. "Yep. I think I got to the bottom of them, though."

"That's good," he said, eyes on the blood going into the vial, not my face.

"And then I spent way too long looking up book stuff on the aether before falling back asleep." (That's the proper name for the internet now—the aether.)

He laughed. "I shouldn't be surprised that the girl with a Shakespearean name loves books."

I was surprised he knew my name was from Shakespeare, though not surprised that Shakespeare is still known. Nerissa is not exactly a main character from a popular play (thanks a lot, Mom and Dad). "Books and music," I said. "Which reminds me, how can I get music from the aether?"

"Ask Chris," he said. "I'm not exactly an aether person."

"A Luddite, even in this day and age!" I crowed.

"A what?" he said. "Never mind. Really, just a snob," he clarified. "I like to think I'm better than everyone else by disdaining their enjoyments." He pulled the vial away. "There! All done. Go get some breakfast and then start preparing for this stupid landing party."

I gave him a sloppy salute. "Aye aye, sir."

"We don't do that in the AEF," he said.

I didn't want to just leave, but I wasn't sure what to say, or even why I wanted to say anything. Finally, I settled on, "By the way, you haven't told me how much you love my hair."

"That's right, I haven't," he agreed, and went back to his desk. It wasn't much, but it was enough for me to smile and head for the door.

"Nerissa," he said at the last minute. "If you have a bad night again—I know you said you've got it under control now, but just in case—call me. Doesn't matter how late. I'll be here."

I won't, but I appreciated him offering, even if it was just a doctor thing. "Thanks," I said.

He gave me half a smile, and then I managed to find my way to the mess, where I had a very late breakfast and got stared at by half the crew, and then escaped back to my quarters to do yet more studying on the last 500 years of history while trying to undo the excited-nervous knots formed in my stomach at the thought of setting foot on an alien world.

This universe, in this time, is *fascinating*.

Wednesday, Later.

I asked Sapphira if it would be OK for me to bring this journal with me to the planet, so I could write down things as they happened instead of trying to hold on to all my first impressions and write them down after getting back to the ship. She said she thought it would be an excellent idea to have an unofficial record from a civilian's point of view.

I stared at her with horror. "Do you mean you're going to want me to *show* this to people?"

"No, no," she assured me. "Not unless you want to. But if you did want to write something for other people to read, having your initial thoughts already down would be useful, don't you think?"

So here I am, writing down my unvarnished impressions.

I am miserable.

Oh, this is fascinating and exciting and thrilling, sure enough—and I'll write down what I think of the planet itself and what has happened since we landed once I get all this off my chest—but underneath my geeking out over alien! planet! I'm positively soaking in angst.

I am so useless here.

They all—everyone else among the landing party—are so efficient. They know exactly what they're doing, and why, and they are trained and prepared for every eventuality, and performing their tasks expertly, and I'm just stumbling around with wide eyes trying to put it all into poetry.

I'm a putterer, and I always have been. In some ways, that was my defense against having two sisters who were so much better than me at everything important: I just stopped caring. I write music, sure, but it's only because of Sarah's urging and Andrew's encouragement that I put out my album a couple years ago. Left to my own, I would have just kept occasionally performing in coffee shops and mostly playing for myself.

I've always believed that I belong in the shadows. Mira and Roz, their natural place is in the sun. Andrew, too, my lovely golden boy. I was content to rustle along behind, mostly overlooked, slipping through life without making much of an impact. Oh, I told myself that my music was important because "The world needs beauty," but even I didn't believe it contributed that much to the sum total of human accomplishment or reflecting the wonder of the Great Creator. I was mostly content with that. Or so I told myself.

Here, though ...

If I had woken up 500 years in the future *on Earth*, I could still putter my way through. Maybe. Things have changed so much, even that's not guaranteed. This ship, though, it's so small, and the mission so big, that everyone here is an expert, highly trained, and so focused on their tasks. There's no room here for a putterer. No room for someone who only wants to drift through life. I can't get away with telling myself that what I do doesn't matter, because there's always someone else who will do it better, when *I am the one here*.

What am I doing here? What's the *point*?

What, if it comes down to it, am I doing in my life at all, even aside from this insane trip into a parallel future? What's the point of me, of Riss? What good am I?

Sheesh. You'd think I would have worked through all this angst when I was a teenager, but I was so busy then building up a shell against Roz and Mira that I kind of skipped over this sort of existential crisis.

I spent too long wallowing in misery here; it's time to turn in and I still haven't written down anything of substance about the planet itself. I'll have to wake up early tomorrow morning to do that.

It is pretty incredible to think about the fact that I am going to sleep on an alien planet, and if I wake up in enough time, I will get to see an alien sun rise over the horizon. All my feelings of inadequacy can't cancel that out.

Thursday, April 30, 2016/Day Eight.

I didn't get a tremendous amount of sleep last night, but I don't feel overtired this morning; rather, sort of fizzy. I got up and crept out of our prefab shelter (it collapses and fits into a tinier bag than I would have ever believed possible) just in time to see the sun rise.

It looks smaller than Earth's sun (though Tyler says that in reality it is bigger and hotter, and it looks smaller because the planet's orbit is further away), and the lights streaking the white sky as it rose were blue and and violet and almost black before they faded and the sky returned to its (apparently) normal bleached white hue.

It was absolutely incredible. I sat and stared, probably with my mouth hanging open. Tyler had also woken up early and joined me. He sighed happily once the light show was finished.

"I've seen half a dozen worlds that are not my own," he said. "It never gets old." He tilted his head and grinned at me. "I'm glad you were here to experience this one."

"It doesn't seem real," I said. "I keep waiting for someone to explain to me how it's all done with CGI and Photoshop." I considered for a moment. "On the other hand, there's a way in which it is more absolutely real than anything else I've ever experienced. I can't explain it."

He rested a hand on my shoulder. "No need."

This entire planet—or as much of it as we explored yesterday—is incredible. The vegetation looks like the best parts of New England in October, but it is as warm and humid as summer in Florida. The most brilliant oranges, deep reds, vibrant golds, trees tall and thin and foofy on top, short puffballs of bushes, long twisty vines creeping over everything, these jagged black mountains stabbing into the white sky way off in the distance ... Sarah would be freaking out to paint it right now. The grass itself is a dull red, rather than green. There's a giant body of water near here, smaller than an ocean but bigger than even a Great Lake. The scientists tested t yesterday, and said its salinity content was comparable to that of the Dead Sea back on Earth. We haven't found any fresh water yet, and also no animal life (probably because of no fresh water).

If you scrape away at the grass and dirt, a short way down you find the ground is solid rock, the same glossy black of the distant mountains.

Like I said: incredible.

Our party consists of two security officers (standard landing party procedure); Sapphira; Tyler; two scientists (also standard procedure for a new world); and me. It's usually six per party; I'm the extra. Sapphira hasn't said anything about Captain Miles's or Dr. Egghead's opinions on my inclusion, and I'm not asking.

Sapphira piloted the shuttle to the surface. The rule is to always have a good pilot in case we need to make a quick getaway.

"Er ... does that happen often?" I asked when they explained this to me at the start of the trip.

"Hardly ever," Tyler said.

"Once in a while," Sapphira tossed over her shoulder as she expertly guided the shuttle through the atmospheric turbulence.

"There was this one time ..." Security Person 1 said.

"And then I remember once ..." Security Person 2 added.

I sat back on the padded bench-like seat, crossed my arms across my chest, and smirked. I can tell when I'm being taken for a ride, literally and metaphorically. I let them tell me their hair-raising stories, and felt better. Surely if it was as dangerous as all that, they wouldn't boast about it so much. If they'd hurried to reassure me, *then* I might have started panicking.

The security people disembarked first, checking the surrounding area with their little hand-held scanning devices. Once they declared it safe, the scientists tripped over each other to get off next.

"It's a competition," Tyler whispered in my ear. "They get five points for each new planet they set foot on; ten points for being the first scientist to walk on it. Whoever has the most points by the time we get back to Earth wins the Most Nerdy trophy."

Sapphira cast an amused glance at us. "I think it has more to do with personal prestige," she said. "They get back to Earth and get to brag about being the first scientist to walk on more worlds than anyone else."

Tyler shook his head. "As a pick-up line, it needs work."

Sapphira locked the shuttle down, and then she, Tyler, and I stepped out.

You are setting foot on an alien world, I told myself. *This is your real life. This is not a dream, not a book you are reading, not a television show. Don't miss a moment! Pay attention, experience everything!*

Of course, I was so focused on not missing anything that I couldn't even let myself feel any natural sensations from walking on a brand-new planet. Then I started scolding myself, and for a few moments I was in real danger of having this incredible experience be ruined by my own stupid brain.

I was saved by Tyler, who looked at me and winked. "How about it, Riss?"

I grinned. My brain settled back down, and I looked around and soaked in the moment.

I felt an echo of the same *wrongness* that had first assailed me when I saw Vreean, Ru-El, and Tyler. My experience tried to tell me that this was impossible, that the way the ground felt beneath my boots (Captain Miles agreed to allow me to use some of the nano-spray we use for underthings to shape some basic footwear. It's thin and slightly uncomfortable, but better than bare feet); the sharp, dry scent to the air and the way it scoured my lungs, the parchment color of the sky and the blue hue to the sun, the odd colors and spindly shapes of the vegetation, the lack of any sound but our voices and the constant soughing of the wind, simply couldn't be real.

When one's senses fight with one's logic, it's a dizzying experience. I bent over, hands on my knees, and drew in two or three gasping breaths. The air caught in my throat, I coughed, and something about that utterly natural and normal act grounded me.

"All right?" Sapphira asked.

I nodded. "It's ... I've no words."

"We'll explore today, sleep here tonight, and fly to the other side of the planet tomorrow," she said.

"And eventually quarter it," Tyler finished. "North, South, East, West. SOP."

Standard Operating Procedure. Even I know that abbreviation.

The exploration took up the rest of the afternoon, and if I am being perfectly honest (which, since this is my private journal and not something I am recording for other people to read, I ought to be) was almost boring for me. Hence the existential crisis yesterday. Everyone else had something to do, some task for which they were uniquely qualified, some reason for being on the landing team.

Me, I wandered around going "Ooh, pretty," and not even knowing why there weren't any signs of animal life.

Ignorance gets old after a while.

The others are starting to wake up now, emerging from the shelter like clowns from a too-small car. I think I'll offer to make breakfast, since cooking is one thing I can do somewhat well. We had ration bars last night for our supper, but surely they'll want something more today ...

Oh. Never mind. Sapphira handed out flat packages which, when one pushes a button on the end, re-hydrates and cooks the food inside. It tastes disgusting, but it is easy and convenient, and then the packaging breaks down into fine ash when you've finished.

I'm not even needed as a *cook*.

The scientists have only a little more to do here, some more samples to collect and the like, and then we fly to the other side of the planet. I don't know much about its rotational pattern, what the seasons are like or anything like that. I asked Tyler, and he told me to wait and see.

"If it's told you, you will forget it," he said. "If you discover it for yourself, you'll always have it."

"Thank you, Socrates," I said sourly.

Alanna Merrill, one of the scientists and an Arethran, told me about a planet discovered a few years back by a mission she was part of, that wobbles so much the seasons can change hourly, or daily, or sometimes go months without changing at all.

"Sucks to be a weatherman on that planet," I said.

Merrill chortled instead of giving me that blank stare I'm getting used to receiving from people when I make what seems like a perfectly ordinary joke to me but has no frame of reference for the people here, so that was nice. They're all understanding about our differences, but it does get lonely. When (if) get back to my own time, I'll have much more sympathy for expats and immigrants.

Thursday, Later.

In the shuttle, flying over the sharp black mountains. Merrill and the other scientist, an alien named Nriin, are arguing incessantly. (I don't know what the name of Nriin's people is - all I know is that Nriin is neither male nor female, has an exoskeleton, and breathes nitrogen so has to wear an oxygen mask, except for nitrogen instead of oxygen, at all times.) Merrill insists it's too dangerous to land in our planned spot, that the readings they're getting from the shuttle scanners indicate the area is unstable. Nriin, who has a communicator built into its mask so that it can talk to us, says that she's being too cautious, and that they didn't volunteer to come on this mission to be safe.

"I'm not saying we should give up all together and return to *Caledonia*," Merrill said, throwing her hands in the air. "I think we should land in a different place, that's all. One with safer readings."

"But if we do not explore the unstable areas, our knowledge of this planet will be incomplete. Sensor readings can only tell us so much. We must view it in person."

"Fine, we'll view it in person, but let's not park the shuttle there, hmm?"

"If we land in the spot you have indicated," leaning forward and tapping one chitinous finger on the map currently glowing on the side viewscreen, "we will lose much time in walking to and from the unstable areas. My calculations indicate that though the area is, as you have pointed out, unstable, the instability is not enough to warrant such a waste of our limited time here."

The conversation got technical after that, and I lost track.

Sapphira, I think, leans toward Merrill's point of view, while Tyler is on Nriin's side. Ultimately, Nriin is the senior scientist on the mission, and so has the final call.

We're going to land.

Sapphira, as pilot, will stay in the shuttle so as to be able to quickly take off if the area proves to be as unsafe as Merrill believes it to be. She (Sapphira, not Merrill) is Thoroughly Unhappy with this turn of events, but because this is a ground mission, the scientists are the bosses, and she has to do what Nriin orders.

(I knew this two chains of command was a bad idea.)

Tyler, the two security people, I, and the scientists will go explore, with the understanding that we will evacuate immediately to the shuttle if anything goes wrong, like earthquakes or lava or mountain giants awakening and trying to eat us.

I confess: I'm a little nervous. I'd feel ten times safer if Sapphira was coming with us. I have unconditional faith in her ability to conquer anything, be it a natural disaster or a human (or alien) one. My faith in Tyler is a little shakier, and pretty much nonexistent in the others. And the fact that Merrill has gone *on record* as saying she thinks this is a bad idea only heightens my tension.

On the other hand . . I'm 500 years in the future, in a parallel universe, on a spaceship, with aliens, and I'm exploring a dangerous planet nobody from the Alliance has ever stepped on before.

There's a tiny part of me that's tap-dancing inside and screaming "Woo-hoo!"

Friday, May 1, 2016/Day Nine.

Somebody needs to slap me the next time I say "Woo-hoo," be it internal or external. Maybe even slap me if I look like I'm thinking it. Never, never again.

Ahem. Yesterday.

We landed in our appointed spot and all of us save Sapphira exited the shuttle. Immediately I could understand Merrill's concern. The ground shook underfoot, constantly, little tremors that felt more like vibrations than an earthquake (well, I assume earthquakes don't feel like that. I've never actually lived through one). The others couldn't feel it until I pointed it out and they knelt down to place their hands on the ground (no dirt or grass here, just pockmarked black rock). Because I'm wearing thin-soled nano-boots, my feet are more sensitive to touch and temperature.

Merrill muttered to herself, but lost some of her concern when Nriin snapped at her to start taking notes. The ruling passion for a scientist—note-taking.

(That and proving each other wrong—but I'm getting ahead of myself.)

The rest of us spread out, everyone from *Caledonia* doing whatever is was they were supposed to do, while I wandered aimlessly and gaped.

We'd flown over the mountains, and everything on this side of them was rock. No trees, no bushes, no grass, no vegetation anywhere, just rock. And another large body of water, which Nriin was making its way toward to test whether it was salt or fresh.

It sounds really bleak, written down like this. And it was ... but there was a beauty to it, as well, even more than the other side. To me, anyway. The dull black rock with sharp edges, the white sky with the whiter sun setting in it, the rippled water reflecting back that parched sky ... it was a study in contrasts, and without all the *wrong* shapes and colors to jangle my mind, I could appreciate it more. If I could paint, I would have wanted to paint this.

A poem was struggling to form itself in my mind, so I quit wandering and sat down on a smooth boulder, leaning forward with my forearms on my knees, staring mostly blankly at the water while my mouth soundlessly shaped words.

Then Tyler appeared at my side. "Stay close to me, will you Riss?" he asked, eyes flickering all around. The setting sun silhouetted his figure, leaching the color from his usually glimmering flesh, transforming him into nothing more than an animated statue wearing clothes. I shivered.

"What's wrong?"

He moved to one side, and I could make out his features again, turning him back into *Tyler*, the person. "I'm starting to lean toward Sapphira and Merrill's point of view," he answered. "I don't like this place."

"Your sensor readings?" I asked.

He shook his head, such a human gesture striking me as odd from someone so alien for the first time. How long had he lived amongst humans to have picked up all their mannerisms? "My instincts," he said. "Nothing I can use to convince Nriin we should go, but they've never failed me yet. I'd feel marginally better about all this if you're with me instead of far off and exposed. In fact, I don't suppose you'd be willing to go back to the shuttle and wait with Sapphira?"

I didn't want to, but worse than being useess would be being the idiot who endangers herself and everyone around her because she's trying to prove something, so I slid off the boulder and walked across the shaking ground toward the shuttle.

I was only halfway there when the planet exploded.

It didn't really explode (or else I wouldn't be writing this now), but that's what it seemed like at the time. Steam burst straight up from every dimple in the rock with as much force as water from a fire hose. I was lucky; remembering games from childhood of avoiding cracks in the sidewalk, I had been stepping between the pockmarks instead of on them. Since it shot straight into the air, I was surrounded by it, but didn't catch any of it myself. My feet did start to burn through the soles of my boots as the ground grew hot and my face felt half-scalded, but that was nothing compared to what it could have been.

Tyler had leaped onto the very boulder I'd been sitting on the instant the ground erupted, and crouched there like a shiny insect, safe from the steam. One of the security people had been climbing a large pile of fallen rock, and so was also safe. Nriin was at the pebbled shoreline of the water, where no steam burst forth.

Merrill and Security Person 2 weren't so lucky.

Security Person 2 was knocked off his feet by the steam, landing with his back and one arm fully in two more jets. He managed to curl in on himself, whereupon he lay there in a tiny ball, moaning.

Merrill's must have been standing directly on a dimple when it happened. The steam blasted her off her feet, sending her through the air to land in a crumpled heap several feet away. Her scream tore through my ears and into my heart.

This all takes time to write out, but of course it happened in the briefest of seconds. In one eyeblink, we went from a happy group on a school outing to victims in a disaster movie. Only Merrill's screams made it obvious that this was real, not special effects.

Tyler stood up on the boulder, balancing precariously, and waved his arm to get everyone's attention who was able to give attention.

"Martou, go to Smith and carry him to the shuttle. Nriin, you and I will get Merrill. Riss, get to the shuttle now!"

"I want to help!" I shouted back, even as Martou (Security Person 1) scrambled down from her safe perch to pick her away across the deadly landscape toward Smith (Security Person 2).

"NO," Tyler said.

One word, but it had its intended effect. I turned away from the injured people and tip-toed my way through and around the jets of steam still coming from the ground, my heart a leaden lump in my chest.

"Faster!" Tyler bellowed, whether at me or the others I couldn't tell. Either way, I obediently picked up my pace as much as I could without running the risk of tripping and planting my face in a steam bath.

An ominous rumbling sound filled the air, and suddenly I found I could indeed move even faster than I already was.

I made it to where Sapphira had already lifted off from the ground and stared helplessly at the open hatch a few feet above my head. There was no way I could leap up to catch that.

Then a ladder clattered down, something more stable than a rope ladder but nowhere near so secure as stairs. Still, it was better than nothing, and I couldn't stand around all day waiting for someone big and strong to come pick me up and throw me into the shuttle. I gulped, grabbed the bottom rung, and climbed.

It was awful—I was sure with each step that I was going to fall and land in the steam—but finally my head drew level with the doorway. I grabbed the blessedly solid lip and dragged myself inside, gasping with exertion and terror.

"Riss?" Sapphira called. She sat at the controls, holding the shuttle steady above the steam.

I drew in an enormous breath. "Yes," I rasped back, my throat gone scratchy from the heat.

"Pull the ladder up and hang on," she said. "I'm moving in to pick up the oth—"

The end of her sentence was lost as the rumbling that had so frightened me earlier built to a climax and the lake erupted.

Nriin, closest to the water, was swept away instantly, a tiny green figure lost against suddenly black water. I think I screamed then. Behind me, Sapphira spat out a short, sharp word that I could tell just from the sound was a vicious curse, and the shuttle picked up speed. I nearly fell out as she veered around and dove as close as she could safely manage toward the ground.

We reached Smith first, and I tossed the ladder over the edge. He sat up and grabbed it with his uninjured arm, but couldn't pull himself up, and Martou, though racing as fast as she could to get to him and away from the towering wall of water that loomed above us, starting to curl in on itself and threatening to fall, was still too far away.

"I'm g-going down to help him," I stuttered to Sapphira, even though the thought of climbing back down into that shriveled me inside.

"No!" she said, almost as sharply as Tyler.

"We have to do something!" I shouted, hating myself for being so useless and only able to take it out on her.

"Get up here," she ordered, and I did, because what else could I do?

The shuttle's controls resembled the yoke of a fighter jet. "Grab that," she said. "And hold it steady. *I'll* go help Smith."

I gaped. "I can't fly this thing!"

"You don't have to fly it, just keep it off the ground," she answered.

There was no time to argue, and besides, one did not argue with Sapphira when she looked like that, all blazing authority and supreme confidence. At least, I didn't. I slid into the seat as she stood up and took the yoke from under her hands. She let go and ran for the ladder.

Immediately as she did, it tried to buck and strain away from me. It really, really wanted to nosedive into the ground. I braced my feet against the bottom of the control panel and pulled back with all my might, struggling to keep it steady. I wasn't entirely successful—I could hear Sapphira swearing steadily as the ladder jerked and spun around while she climbed—but we didn't crash.

In less time than I would have believed possible, she made it back into the shuttle, Smith draped over one shoulder. Following hard on her heels was Martou, panting and white-faced.

Sapphira didn't even stop to wipe the sweat off her face; she came back to the cockpit and took the yoke back from me. I swear the stupid thing purred when it felt an expert's hands controlling it again.

"Go help," she said, jerking her head back to where Martou was trying to tend Smith's injuries while still perched at the open hatch in order to drop the ladder to Tyler and Merrill.

I think it was then that my brain shut off and my body went into automatic. Back I went, to move Smith as carefully as possible away from the hatch and follow Martou's barked orders about gauze and ointment in the emergency medical kit. I was not aware of anything else until Tyler's head appeared above the lip to the hatch. As Sapphira had done with Smith, he carried Merrill over one shoulder and settled her as gently as possible on the floor before climbing in himself. The instant he was inside, Martou pulled the ladder up and slapped the control to close the door.

"Go go go!" she shouted at Sapphira, who pulled the shuttle up so sharply we all tumbled toward the back.

"It's about to blow," Martou said, staring out the viewscreen.

I followed her gaze, and understood why neither Sapphira nor Tyler had been willing to let me slow them down by helping.

The steam had only been a precursor. Even as the wave of water broke down over the land, fire erupted from every pore of the ground. Water and fire mixed together, boiling and steaming, in some parts the fire streaking the water with tongues of flame.

It was an awe-inspiring sight, and a terrifying one when I thought that if we'd been five seconds slower, that would have overwhelmed all of us.

"What about Nriin?" I whispered, even as my hands were busy wrapping Merrill's legs while Tyler worked on her upper half. It was easier to look at the horror outside than the horror that was her body.

Tyler stopped and put his head in his hands.

"There's a chance it might have survived," Sapphira said, her voice remarkably steady. "Those exoskeletons are amazing. As soon as it calms down, we'll start scanning for life signs."

Merrill, burned as she was, stirred. "I ... told ... it ... so," she moaned, and then fainted.

Scientists!

We are back aboard the *Caledonia* now. Or, well, some of us are. Dr. Selby met us in the shuttle bay and hustled Smith and Merrill to sickbay without so much of a glance at the rest of us, muttering under his breath the entire time. Oddly enough, this actually served to make me feel marginally better. It seemed so *normal*, as if nothing out-of-the-ordinary or truly terrifying were happening. They left me here, too, picked up some more useful people, and then Sapphira, Tyler, and Martou took the shuttle back down to search for Nriin or for Nriin's body. If even that survived the fiery deluge.

I'm shamefully glad to be safely back, tucked away in my little cabin writing all this down with as much detail as I can in case they do need my notes for the report (I'll obviously edit out all the personal bits). At the same time, I honestly do wish I was back there with them. I wasn't injured, so I *should* be there, seeing this through to the end.

That's nonsense, of course, and the practical part of me knows it. There is no way that I should take up space in the shuttle that could instead go to someone valuable, someone who could mean the difference between rescuing Nriin or—or not. I know that. And yet I still feel like a slacker, a coward, holed away here while others clean up the mess.

Mostly, I guess, I just feel miserable that I can't be that useful person helping to rescue Nriin. Darn it, when people like me end up on adventures like this, we're supposed to turn out to be heroes! The one who saves the day, who pulls out previously undiscovered skills that rescue everyone. You know, the *Chosen One*. That's how it works in all the books and movies, why not for me?

Instead, the best I could manage was keeping the shuttle from crashing entirely while everyone else did the hard work.

Which is *something*, I suppose. At least I *didn't* crash the shuttle. And at least I didn't need rescuing. That would have been the absolute worst. Ugh.

Someone's at my door. It's too soon for Sapphira and the rest to be back, isn't it?
—It's Dr. Selby.

Friday, Later.

That was ... interesting.

I was afraid, when Selby showed up unexpectedly, that he was here to tell me that Merrill or Smith, or both of them, had died. But when he came in and leaned against the doorframe without saying a word, I deduced he must have come by for something else. (I know, I'm a regular Sherlock Holmes.)

"Why aren't you in sickbay?" he began.

"Hello to you too," I said, letting out a breath I hadn't realized I was holding. He wouldn't be that cranky if there was trouble.

He didn't do anything so obvious as grin, but a little light flickered in his eyes at my response. "You do realize that after what you went through down there on Planet Hell you need to be checked over?"

"I'm fine, Doctor," I said. "My arms are a little sore from piloting the shuttle, that's all." I paused for a moment, thinking. "And my feet ache."

His face pinched together. "And you're a professional, able to diagnose medical issues simply based on how you feel at the moment, are you?"

"No," I said, unable to keep bantering. "No kind of professional at all."

He peered at me for a moment, then came further into the room and sat down at my desk. "All right," he said. "Spill."

"You're not going to try to make me talk about my feelings, are you?" I parried.

He snorted. "Feelings are not part of my job description, thank goodness."

I didn't have any clever reply to make to that. He just sat there, watching me as I huddled on my little seat beneath the porthole, and then, I found myself talking.

"I was so useless down there," I said quietly, gazing out at the pinpricks of starlight piercing the darkness. "I'm useless here in general. And—I don't know, it sounds stupid, but I just—I want to make an impact. I want to matter." Andrew had mattered. When Andrew had died, huge holes opened up not only in my life, but the lives of all who knew him. Why couldn't it work that way for me? "But I know that if—when—I leave here, I won't leave a gap. You'll all make a note in your reports, and the Advent of Riss will just be one more slightly interesting thing to have happened on your search for new worlds."

He raised one eyebrow. "Is that really what you think?"

I swallowed and leaned my head against the porthole, welcoming the coolness of the glass (not really glass, I know) against my cheek. "I suppose not," I admitted. "No. That's self-pity talking."

He gave an exaggerated sigh. "Thank goodness I don't have to tell you that."

"Sorry," I said. "I know the last person I should be thinking about now is myself."

"Will you quit doing that?" he said.

I sat up. "Doing what?"

"Apologizing all the time. Thanking people for basic courtesy. Acting as though you don't have any right to … to have feelings, or exist. I get that you don't want to talk about your feelings. Trust me, I understand that. But that doesn't mean you don't deserve to have any. It was terrible down there, and not something you've ever experienced before. Of course it would shake you up. I'd be worried about you if it didn't. So stop being so damned apologetic."

I wasn't sure whether to laugh, cry, or throw something at him. In the end, I just spoke, without censoring myself for a change.

"When I—when Andrew—with my husband, I knew I was valued," I said. "For the first time in my life, I was with someone who didn't make me feel like I had to earn his love. With him, I could be 'just Riss,' and that was enough. I've never felt that way apart from him. Before we met, and then after he died, I ... I struggle to believe that I ... it's hard for me to think I have any worth in and of myself, much less believe that others can see that in me. Coming here, that just reinforces it. I know in my head it isn't true, but my heart doesn't like to listen." I paused and swallowed. This wasn't easy to get out.

"I'm a putterer," I said. "Always have been. And I just ... I just don't want to be useless my entire life. I want to *live*, instead of sitting on the sidelines watching everyone else's lives." Or singing about them.

I just don't know how to start living.

"Nerissa," Selby said, then stopped and cleared his throat. "Riss." He stopped again and shook his head. "No, I can't make it work. Nerissa," he said more definitively.

Even in the midst of my turmoil, I couldn't keep a small smile from my face. "Doctor Selby."

"What you do has nothing to do with who you are," he began, then stopped one more time, frowning thoughtfully. "No, that's not quite right. They are connected, but you're still wrong."

"Thank you," I said.

He ignored this. I leaned back against the wall while waiting for him to sort his thoughts, and wished I had some sort of throw I could pull over my lap. My fingers played restlessly with each other in the silence. It took conscious effort to still them. Selby, naturally, could sit in perfect stillness and silence and not seem remotely bothered.

At last, his face cleared and he spoke again. "Got it! You are basing your value on what you do, but it's the other way around. Who you are affects what you do."

"Great, so you're saying I'm a putterer because I'm naturally deficient?" That sounded exactly like the sort of thing Roz and Mira said to me and about me all the time, that if you'd just exert a little more *effort*, Rissy ... Why had I thought I could trust him, that I could be honest with him? Just because he'd been kind and understanding, and had apologized the one time he treated me like less than a person?

He slashed his hand down through the air. "No, no, no! First of all, what's wrong with being a putterer? What's the matter with enjoying life, and people, and not feeling like you've always got to be striving for greatness?"

That was a viewpoint that had never occurred to me. It was certainly one never endorsed by anyone in my entire extended family.

"Second of all ..." he leaned forward, eyes intense, "You are looking to find your worth in what you do. That's too crushing a weight to put on anyone's shoulders, and it's a false valuing anyway. Even if you were paralyzed and incapable of communication, you would still have value, Nerissa. Because your value is based on *you*, on who you are, not on what you do." He stood up from his chair. "Get that straightened out in your head, and you might just find that you are able to have some purpose in your life after all. You never know. In the meantime, come to sickbay so I can make sure you didn't take a blow to your head down there."

It wasn't a pretty speech. It was blunt and forceful, and stopped just short of saying *get a grip, Nerissa*. And yet, it was the best thing I could have heard. As I write this down now, after he's gone back to sickbay (after extracting a promise from me that yes, I would come by and get checked), I can remember each word with perfect clarity. Not like some of the conversations I have with people, where I can write down the general gist of what we all said but have to fill in some of the details myself.

I think even if I weren't to write it down, I'd always remember.

I was right to trust him after all.

And now I suppose I'd better get to sickbay to keep my promise.

Saturday, May 2, 2016/Day Ten.

They found Nriin.

It's a mess, but still alive. Barely.

I can't even begin to imagine how they got it out.

Dr. Selby and his staff are working non-stop to save its life.

I keep having flashbacks to being in the hospital while the doctors were working on Andrew.

Wish there was a chapel on board.

Saturday, Later.

Nriin died this afternoon.

Merrill is recovering, but Smith has developed an infection, and Selby's not sure he can save him.

This time travel adventure suddenly seems a lot less adventurous, and a lot more horrible.

Saturday, Later Yet.

We lost Smith, too.

Monday, May 4, 2016/Day Twelve.

This is awful. I feel so sick. My own problems of needing "meaning" and "purpose" in my life seem a whole lot less relevant in light of all this. Time to stop *talking* about wanting to do something meaningful with my life, and actually live it. Less thinking about what a looooser I am, and more acting with and for other people.

So I stuffed my horror of deathbeds and near-deathbeds down somewhere near my toes last night, and went and sat with Merrill for a while in sickbay, because I thought she could use some company. I don't know that it was all that helpful, but it was better than sitting in my cabin whimpering.

Then Tyler collected me and he, Sapphira, Martou, and I commandeered a table in the mess to ourselves, and worked together to write out the report for our trip to what we're now all calling Planet Hell. My journal did come in handy there, although I was careful not to let anyone else read it.

Mark Danvers joined us toward the end. He was a real mess; he and Merrill are good friends, and he and Nriin had been close. I guess all the scientists are shaken up by this—usually if someone's going to get killed on a mission it's the AEF people, not the scientists—and Mark's been hit especially hard. I sat and talked with him, listened, really, while he talked, even after the others left. He seemed to appreciate it. I thought it was the least I could do.

There's a part of my mind that keeps wanting to think *If only I was smarter, or stronger, or faster, I could have done something to help, maybe I could have saved them*, but I'm doing my best to shut it off every time it pipes up.

<u>This isn't about me.</u>

We had a joint memorial service this morning. Captain Miles said some really good things about Smith; I may not like the man, but he cares for his people. Dr. Eggleston mumbled a little bit for Nriin. I wish Mark could have spoken for it. I try not to be prejudiced against Eggleston because the guy treats me like dirt, but he acted like he barely cared for Nriin at all. It's entirely possible, I suppose, that he cares too much about the people working under him to be able to speak fluently when he loses one. But

Captain Miles wasn't fluent, and was in fact his usual stiff and formal self, and you could still see how badly he felt about Smith's death. So I don't think it's just my personal dislike for Eggleston that makes me think he is a jerk to everyone, including his own scientists.

I went back to sickbay after the service to sit with Merrill. She'd watched it through the ship-wide communication system, but it still bothered her that she couldn't be there for it.

"I should have pushed harder," she mumbled. The flesh around her mouth is still healing, and talking is difficult for her, but I think staying silent would be impossible. "I should have convinced Nriin that it wasn't safe for us there. I should have reasoned more from the data, I should have …"

I searched for something to say. I remember how much well-meaning cliches hurt me after Andrew died. I didn't want to tell her it wasn't her fault, or that there was no point in beating herself up. She knew that. Knowing doesn't change how you feel, though.

How many times have I had to tell myself that there was no way for me to know the car accident was going to happen, that it was the fault of the other driver having the sun in his eyes, that it had nothing to do with me, that I couldn't have prevented it even if I'd been there?

Countless, and yet I still feel guilt over the fact that he drove off to work that morning without me in the car, and he died and I lived.

So in the end, I didn't say anything to Merrill, just sat beside her and let her mumble her self-reproaches, and stayed like that until Mark came to sit with her for a while.

I'm trying to find a way to talk to Selby, or at least be there for him if he wants to talk. He looked awful at the service. Losing two patients like that—I can't imagine. He's been so good to me; I would like to be able to do the same for him. He hasn't been in sickbay the last couple of times I stopped by. I'll have to ask Lieutenant Allain (the junior med officer) about him. I understand if he doesn't want to be around people—oh boy do I understand—but I also don't want him to think nobody cares about him, or sees that he's suffering too.

* * *

Monday, Later.

Back from finally tracking Selby down.

Lt. Allain seemed uncomfortable telling me anything about his boss (understandable), so I went to Sapphira instead.

She's handling the deaths better than any of the rest of us from the mission. "It's horrible, but you learn to brace yourself for it," she told me. "The first time you're on a mission gone wrong is the worst. After that, you're always prepared for it to end in disaster, and it's a happy surprise when it doesn't."

Maybe she's right, but I don't think I could ever grow that tough a skin.

Anyway, she listened to me stumble through my explanation of why I was looking for Selby, and told me his cabin number without any commentary when I finished.

I felt supremely awkward when I stood in front of the door and knocked. Was this the right thing to do? What if he slammed the door in my face? (If they can slam doors here—the vanishing and reappearing thing seems to preclude that.) Would it look weird, me showing up at his cabin like that? What if he thought ... well, that my motives were, *ahem,* less than pure?

(I'm blushing like crazy just writing that.)

Then the door melted away, and he stood there in its place glaring at me out of bloodshot eyes, and I stopped worrying. He so obviously needed *someone*.

"My turn to ask if you want to talk," I said with a wry smile.

He stared at me for a moment, then stood back. "Come in."

His cabin, being further from the nose, is a little bigger, but even more sparse than mine. He doesn't have any art on his walls, his bunk was made with meticulous neatness, and his desk was clear of any personal possessions. If you wanted to gauge Gideon Selby's personality by his home, you'd be out of luck.

He did have an extra chair, and he waved me to that while he slouched spinelessly into his desk chair.

"Rough few days," I said, possibly the understatement of the year.

"You could say that," he replied dryly.

That avenue of conversation seemed at an end. Before I could come up with a better, he spoke.

"I refused to join the navy, or any of the military branches of the Alliance, because I couldn't bear to spend my life patching up people injured in stupid wars, and then send them off to get killed or kill again."

I leaned back in my chair and said nothing.

"I couldn't stay planetside, though." He pushed a hand back through his mussed brown hair, a boyish and endearing gesture. "My mother was a spacer; I inherited her wanderlust. Besides, people annoy me too much for me to stay in one place for long."

I couldn't help a giggle at that; it was so absolutely typical of him. He glanced up, grinned briefly in acknowledgment, and then returned to his tale.

"So I joined the AEF. The pay was better than shipping with some merchants or mercenaries, made my folks proud, and kept me away from war. I *volunteered* for this mission, out of my mind I must have been." He shook his head.

"Not in it for the adventure, then?" I asked.

"Not so much," he said. Then he *squirmed*—(no, honestly, just like a little kid)—and muttered, "If you must know, I was trying to escape my mother's attempts to marry me off. She, er, is starting to get insistent about grandchildren."

It took all my self-control to keep from bursting into laughter. Only the memory of Smith and Nriin, and my reason for visiting Selby in the first place, kept me sober.

He heaved a sigh and returned to his original lament "And now here I am, losing people left and right, just like I was afraid would happen in the military. Such a stupid, stupid reason this was, too—all so they could come home and brag about the pretty new planet they discovered." His voice went high on that last part, as though mimicking a kid.

"Or ..." I said slowly, thinking aloud. "Or you could say that they died so that others, coming through this part of space after us, wouldn't fall victim to the planet."

We both were silent after that.

"Yeah," Selby said. "I guess you could look at it that way." Then he gave me an odd look. "You said us."

"What?"

"You said coming through here after *us*."

I hadn't even realized it.

"Starting to think of yourself as part of the crew, are you?"

"I—don't know," I said.

"You haven't given up hope that you'll get back to your home, have you?"

I had to think about that for a minute. Had I? "I think I've stopped thinking about it," I told him. "There's been too much else happening, and nobody even seems to know how I got here in the first place, and it's obviously not a high priority on the Captain's list, and … I guess if I think about it too much it gets overwhelming, so I try to just keep moving forward."

He nodded. "Sensible of you."

I didn't tell him the other part of it, which I realized only when I started talking.

I'm not so sure I want to go home.

Which is horrible, and I don't even know why I feel that way (which is why I didn't mention it to Selby). I can't think about it right now.

"Well," he said after a few more moments. "Thanks for stopping by, Nerissa."

I stood up. "Sure thing, Doc."

He came to his feet as well. "You know," he said. "You're not part of the Fleet. If you want … you could call me Gideon."

"Gideon," I said, testing it. Then I shook my head. "You can't manage Riss, and I don't think I can make Gideon work. But," I added, "I think I could do Selby."

"Fair enough," he said. He took my hand to shake, and instead held it inside his for a few moments before he seemed to wake up. Without saying anything else, he opened the door for me, and that was the end of that.

I still feel horrible about Nriin and Smith. But I feel calmer overall. And I think I was able to help Selby.

I'm glad of that.

Wednesday, May 6, 2016/Day Fourteen.

Life is starting to return to normal, or for what passes on normal on a space corvette deep in uncharted territory. With a visitor from a parallel universe (presumably) on board, to boot.

We are still waiting to hear back from AEF Command regarding what's to be done with me. It's disconcerting, having my entire future dependent on some strangers who've never met me or know anything about me. I feel I really ought to have some say in the matter. Then again, what *can* I say? "Captain, I insist you drop everything in order to get me back to my own place and time, even though we don't know how I got here and you don't know anything about parallel universes in general and it very well might be impossible."

I know that Mark Danvers and one or two of the other scientists have been working on theories and experiments in their spare time. Dr. Egghead refuses to allow them to do anything while on *his* time, as he still insists parallel universes are a scientific impossibility, and therefore I can only be here on Nefarous Purposes. What a tool. I can't even get down to the science labs to see what they're doing (not that it would make any sense to me, being decidedly un-scientific even in my own time), because he insists I'm Not To Be Trusted. Seriously, you can *hear* the capital letters when he speaks.

Ah well, presumably Mark and the rest will figure out some brilliant way to get me back, and AEF will confirm it, and before I know it I'll be waking up back on my ratty old blue couch two weeks ago, fielding an angry phone call from Roz demanding to know why I ignored her last night when she tried calling.

Ha ha. As if she doesn't know. As if she and Mira haven't been conspiring together to try to guilt me into moving back home.

Oh my word, can you imagine? (Well no, you can't, because you're just a journal, and have no imagination, or brains at all.) It's almost enough to make me want to beg the Captain to let me stay here, yes, even for eight years in space. Mira had called the day before—Tuesday—and did the guilt thing. "Mom and Dad are getting so lonely, they really need their kids, and you know that Roz and I can't drop our lives to go spend time with them every day, and yes I know that you didn't want to make any big changes right after *he* died [my sisters refuse to say Andrew's name since his death], but it's been a year now and you can't wallow forever, you have to start thinking about other people for a change, Rissy."

All of which meant that Roz was going to use the other bludgeon: "You really need to make something of your life, you can't get by on your tiny salary from the bookstore and *his* life insurance forever, and even if you could, now's the perfect time to really pursue your career. You should move back home to cut down on your expenses, and if this music thing is really what you want to do with your life, then you should go after that. Also I could really use a baby-sitter for the kids because our nanny is quitting and I don't have the time to find a new one."

Batter, crash, bang, thump, until my head is spinning and my ears ringing. That Wednesday, the day before I woke up in the pod, had been awful. The last day of the first year of life without Andrew. I'd tried to act as though everything was normal and it was just another day, but oh, was I miserable. When my phone buzzed that evening and showed Roz's number, I knew that I should answer it, that ignoring her would only make things harder later on, but I couldn't do it. I turned my phone off and went to sleep instead. Talking to her would have made me want to run as far and as fast away from everything, from life itself, as I could.

Gah. Enough thinking about this. I'll go back, somehow, and I'll figure out how to deal with Roz and Mira somehow, and the rest of my family with their more subtle ways of trying to control me, and then I'll somehow figure out what I *am* going to do with the rest of my life, now that the path I thought was laid for my feet (wife, mother, amateur musician and book seller) has crumbled to dust.

At least these two weeks here, on this wild adventure, have given me some breathing space, a chance to be the kind of person I could never have been back home. I've started writing poetry again, even if it isn't very good. I stood up to Selby for my own rights. I've kept a shuttle from crashing and mourned together with other people for the loss of life of two of our own.

I'll carry this with me when I go back, and ~~hopefully~~ it will give me strength. It will. It *must*.

Ack! My wall squawked at me. Still not used to this ..

It was Chris. She's coming off duty and wants to know if I'll join her for a meal. Still absurdly pleased when people actually want my company. Trying not to think about how hard it's going to be when I go back home, knowing I'll never see any of them ever again. Wouldn't it be nice if we could figure out a way for me to get back and forth easily, and as much time as I spend here, can still go home to the exact moment I left, every time? My own personal Narnia!

I suppose that would be too much of having my cake and eating it too. After all, even Peter and Lucy and the rest had to leave Narnia for good eventually.

Enough maundering. I have a friend to meet. I don't know how much time I have left here, and I'm not going to waste it all sitting in a cabin by myself.

Thursday, May 7, 2016/Day Fifteen.

Oh man, Captain Miles is seriously pissed at me. I can't even blame him.

AEF Command back on Earth has decided that finding someone from a parallel universe is exactly part of what this deep space mission is all about, and so we have to turn the ship around and go back to where they found me, to see if they can discover the "rift" between universes I came through, and why I came and how, and if it's possible to travel between rifts (The further we get from Earth, the longer it takes for communication to go through, which is why this has taken so long. Well, that and bureaucracy).

The Captain really, really hates turning the ship around. He wants to get so far into deep space that they set a record which will remain unbroken for the next century. In fact, some of the crew suspects that he wouldn't mind if the *Caledonia* never returns to Earth.

Mark Danvers sat down very seriously with me this morning and told me not to get my hopes up about the rift. He said all of their experiments have ended in disaster, and they won't risk my life sending me back through unless they are absolutely certain it will work. He said they might, possibly, be able to get me back to my universe, but not back to my time. Conversely, they might be able to use the rift to send me back in time, but in this universe, not my own. And unless we can do both, what's the point?

I am ... nonplussed. Part of me still feels like ha ha, of course I'll get back, there's no way this is forever. The other part of me has, I think, ever since I arrived here, believed it's for good. I'm mostly not thinking about it one way or another right now.

Dr. Egghead is spitting mad, since he Does Not Believe in parallel universes and is convinced this is all some horrible plot meant to Make Him Look Bad in front of his peers when he gets back to Earth. My heart weeps for him.

Snort

Even if I can't go back, I hope we find answers. I like answers, they are such nice tidy things, and it will be much easier to figure out what to do with my life here in this place once everything is wrapped up from my past. Not like it will magically make everything vanish from my memory, but at least I won't always be wondering: here or there? Past or future?

Although I am very determinedly not thinking about my future if I can't return. Eight years aboard this ship, unless the Captain maroons me on a deserted planet somewhere, and then ... what? Do they have use for my gifts in this time and space? And what do I do aboard the ship in the meantime, just hang around twiddling my thumbs? The disaster on Planet Hell proves conclusively that I don't have a whole lot to offer to the ship (though I'm <u>done</u> angsting about it).

In eight years, I'll be almost forty. What'll I do back on Earth, or any of the planets in the Alliance supposing I don't want to settle on Earth? I doubt there's a place in this era for a musician of an ancient style, with no instrument, or a bookseller in a world where all books are available through the aether. What *can* I do here?

So much for not thinking—or angsting—about it.

One step at a time, Riss. There will be answers soon enough. Maybe I can go back after all, though that thought still doesn't fill me with wild joy, as much as I'm ashamed to admit it. Or if I can't go back, maybe Captain Miles and AEF Command between them will think of something for me to do.

Or maybe I'll grow more than just a hint of a backbone and figure something out on my own. Miracles can happen, right? How else do you explain me getting here in the first place?

Saturday, May 9, 2016/Day Seventeen.

After my bloodwork this morning, Selby sat down and discussed the results from the past few days with me. He says there's no change in my DNA yet, but the Captain wants him to keep checking. I've taken to calling him (Selby, not Miles) a vampire for all the blood he takes. He just does that raised-eyebrow thing in return. It was a pleasantly mature and reasonable conversation between doctor and patient (OK, maybe not the vampire bit), and it's ridiculous that I should want to cry from feeling so respected.

You know, like a *normal* person.

Everything else is fairly calm. We're all still subdued from the disaster on Planet Hell, but also starting to move forward from it. In some ways, I think these new orders regarding Yours Truly are helping; it's giving everyone a new purpose. Mark Danvers is working double-time on theories and what-not regarding the parallel universes, how I might have gotten here, and what to do about it. With the official orders to learn as much as they can about The Rift, even Dr. Egghead can't complain about Mark using his on-duty hours for this. Tyler and his crew of engineers have been set to work stabilizing the engines and making sure the shields are up to snuff, so that we can be close to the rift without getting sucked through.

"Yeah, that would really suck," I said when Tyler told me this, and was absurdly pleased when he burst into genuine laughter over even such a lame pun.

Decidedly, everyone is beginning to heal, even if it will be a long time before the holes left by Nriin and Smith fill.

Chris is more subdued these days—Smith was the first loss of any of "her" people, and she's still not sure how to deal with it. Still, I saw a glimmer of her old self yesterday, when I asked her how to play music on my computer and we chatted for a little about inconsequential things. She wanted to know about fashion and styles back in my time, and I asked her if folk-style music was still popular (spoiler: it isn't), and it was very light and casual.

I've started to get to know more of the crew outside of sickbay, and am thinking about taking Chief Tyler up on his offer to accidentally get lost in engineering.

Space travel, when you have no duties, is decidedly boring.

Never thought I'd get sick of having copious amounts of time to read and no chores to distract me, but I'm going to start pacing the halls—corridors—soon. *I want my guitar.*

Not that even my guitar would do me much good if I do stay, and I do have to adapt to this time. Imagine if a Renaissance composer with a lute showed up to the modern music scene. What I am and do? *Even more outdated.* Music is so, so, sosososo different now from what I'm used to, and I'm not sure I could ever adapt my style to be anything more than a bizarre novelty if I stayed.

Music is immersive now; it's auditory and visual and, in the best pieces, tactile as well. That's right: you see and feel as well as hear it. Which is totally awesome, and I want to experience it and learn how to do it (if I stay), but you have to train from the time you're really, really young to become an expert. To sit down and plunk out a few chords on a guitar while singing a lyric or two? That is so far removed from what they think of as "music" that it might as well be—on a different planet.

Ha ha.

Maybe I can convince Chris to teach me how to shoot those cool ray guns in her off time.

Later.

Chris said no to the guns, but she will start giving me some basic lessons in self-defense. She said that's only common sense.

That's a little more intense than I was hoping for, and more serious, but good, I guess? I do want to be able to defend myself and not have to rely on others, but on the other hand it's kind of freaky to think about needing such skills. And how could I explain me getting buff overnight to the folks back home if I do make it back?

On the other hand again, anything I can do to keep from being a burden to the people here is good. I mean, it wouldn't have helped on Planet Hell (seems like everything I do or think right now circles back to that), but if we were in another dangerous situation, being able to defend myself would be good. And if it keeps me from getting bored (how many hands am I up to now—four?), I'll take it.

Sunday, May 10, 2016/Day Twenty.

Ow.

Sunday, Later.

No, seriously. Ow. Even writing hurts. Whose stupid idea was this self-defense thing anyway?

Tuesday, May 12, 2016/Day Twenty-Two.

I am *so* sore from my first few self-defense lessons with Chris. I am also quite thoroughly terrible at them, but Chris says I have a good instinct, and should get better with practice.

Despite the pain, I actually have enjoyed my two lessons. Now that I've had a few days to think about it, I like the thought of being strong enough to protect myself. I also appreciate the chance to work out my frustrations and fears physically, instead of letting them fester.

Huh. Just remembered Tom trying to talk me into joining a gym after Andrew died. Probably should've listened to him.

Chris called me over to her table when I went to the mess for lunch today. She was sitting with Ona and wanted me to tell her (Ona, not Chris) more about some of the everyday life stuff that's normal for me and that Chris finds hysterically weird.

"Tell her about buses," she ordered.

Public transportation on Earth now involves something called the hoverrail, which sounds like a cross-country subway system, except in the air instead of underground. They still have ground roads for private transportation, but few people bother with them; they are slow and expensive and poorly maintained, so almost everyone relies on the hoverrail. The idea of public buses strikes Chris as the dumbest thing she's ever heard.

Cities also, or at least cities as I know them, are *out there* so far as Chris and the rest of this Earth's inhabitants think. Everything is much more ... organic, from the sound of it. Cities have been grown, not built, with houses and apartments worked into trees (hello, Endor and Lothlorien!) in some places, and everything overall incorporated more as part of the earth, not separate from it. It makes me kind of wistful to hear the others talk about it, because it sounds so much lovelier than the Earth I know. Also hopeful, though, because it turns out we humans are going to eventually learn how to properly steward the world. From what I've learned since my arrival, I can almost understand why Dr. Egghead thinks of us as barbarians, we are so far removed from their idea of anything properly resembling civilized behavior. On the other hand, *he* was completely rude to *me*, which isn't civilized by anyone's standards.

I don't mind it when Chris treats me as a freak show, really. Probably because it's not *me* she's treating as freaky, just the world I come from. She's genuine about it, too, honestly finding it fun and a little bit silly how we lived—live—and not using pseudo-humor to put me down or make me feel like less of a person because I came from such a "weird" time.

That said, I wish she would stop. Every time I start to get used to life here, something else happens to remind of how ... *alien* it all is. Not just the actual aliens, but everything. I could spend the rest of my life trying to grow accustomed to it here, and I still would never truly belong. It would always be *other* for me. Even the language! I'm good at the patois, getting used to it even without the translator, but my ear aches sometimes for plain old English, peppered with jokes and cliches and references I know without having to think about.

The thought of not being able to go back doesn't scare me as much as it probably should. The thought of having to live the rest of my life here is frighteningly lonely. Nobody who understands even the basics of my world, and me constantly tripping over the basics of theirs.

Then again, immigrants have had to deal with that sort of thing for centuries, and many of them were leaving behind way more than I am. So I guess I can't complain that much. My situation may be weirder than theirs, but I'm not really all that special.

Thursday, May 14, 2016/Day Twenty-Four.

We've arrived back at the site of my grand arrival, more quickly than I expected. The Captain pushed to get us here as fast as the *Caledonia* could take us, so we could "finish all this nonsense." At any rate, here we are again. Thankfully with less puking and panicking on my part this time around. They're doing plenty of scans of the area and the scientists are all scowling at the results of said scans, and I keep getting dragged back to sickbay so they can check my DNA and a myriad of other things that might give them clues, and yet I've still not been to the bridge. Over three weeks aboard the *Caledonia*, and I haven't been given the grand tour. All this commotion revolving around me, and they won't even let me on the bridge to see things for myself—and this when I might be leaving soon, too!

I think this is tremendously unfair.

Selby is at least making sure to pass on all information about said DNA and myriad other things. None of it means anything to me, but I appreciate the effort he's making. He seems determined to not fall into the trap of treating me as a test subject again, and I am equally determined to not fall into *my* default of assuming I don't deserve to be treated as a reasonable adult.

It's a lot easier to stay away from that default here. Captain Miles is annoyed with me —no, be fair, Riss. He's annoyed with the situation caused by me being here, but he doesn't treat me as less of a person. Even Dr. Egghead, for all that he loathes me, treats me as much of a person as he does anyone else. That's not saying much, but at least he doesn't give respect to others and demean me.

It's a weird kind of symbiosis—the more I live in a way that deserves respect, the more respect I receive. And the more respect I receive, the easier it is to live deserving of respect.

A dance of mirrors
In a hall that twists.
The reflection is never quite true

But both sides
Make the other better.

All of this that I'm writing is, of course, to distract me from what's to come. Either we don't find out anything, and I'm stuck here as an anomaly without ever knowing what happened to bring me here, or we find out what it was and can't reproduce it so I'm stuck here forever, or I go back and try to rebuild life back in my own time, on my own planet, and let this fade to a memory.

Honestly, none of these options appeal to me. The frustrating thing is, I can't think of what *would*. When I stop to think about what would be the life I want to live, what I want to happen, my mind goes blank.

I suppose that means I need to accept whatever life I'm given, instead of always wishing for something different. That's the pat, proper answer, anyway. I'm a little skeptical of it, but nothing better's occurring to me.

Friday, May 15, 2016/Day Twenty-Five.

I've taken to hanging out in sickbay even when they don't need me for tests, because at least there I can keep somewhat abreast of what they're learning from the debris and the space around it. In my quarters, all I ever hear is "Ms. Waldon to sickbay," and then I can't make any sense out of what they wanted me for.

Selby hasn't said anything about me leaning over his shoulder every time they talk to him over the intercom (or "com" as they call it, because you can't have a ship in deep space without cool-sounding nicknames for all your devices). Not like it's helping me much. I *still* don't understand anything.

I'm beginning to wish I hadn't slept through my science classes in college.

Here's the gist of what I've gathered so far: parallel universes usually look something like this:

////// et cetera.

All running alongside each other (but how? Where? I ask Mark this and his eyes begin to glitter, his skin color shifts from dark brown to indigo, and techno-babble spills out his mouth faster and faster, and I'm left even more confused than I was before. They're just ... somewhere, I guess), but not intersecting. *Except*, theoretically, once every millennia or so, something happens with two universes going side by side, and they touch for just a moment. So then you have:

//X//.

After they touch, they go back to running along their own path.

Me coming over from my universe into this one is the center of the X of these two universes. Mark theorizes that the other-Nerissa has hopped over to my universe when I came to this one, but we still don't know why. He suspects that she went back to the day I left—Thursday, April 24, 2016—but he has no explanation for why I didn't wake up the same day in this universe, why I jumped ahead 500 years, and what happened to make her decide to join the bio-freeze expedition and me not. He keeps saying, "Hopefully we'll learn more when we get to the rift," but he also suspects it might remain one of those things that never gets a full explanation.

"Even science can't answer everything," he said. (Bet Dr. Egghead loved that.)

There's a patch of "weirdness" (Sapphira's phrase, she says that's the technical term) in space around the debris from the failed pods, but they don't dare get too close to examine it, because we don't know what it'll do to the ship. Or what the ship'll do to the weirdness, for that matter.

Tyler and his people have prepared some unmanned probes to check it out. If those slip through a tear in the fabric of reality there won't be a huge impact. We hope.

The parallel lives thing is weird to think about, even more than the parallel universes. Are other-Nerissa and I exactly the same in every way but one? What about our souls? Is there one soul splintered throughout every one of me and my dopplegängers, or do we each have our own? Are we truly individuals, or reflections of each other? Who is the true Nerissa, and are the rest of us shadows? (I mean, obviously I'm the true Nerissa—but what if I'm not?)

When we die, do our souls blend into one, or are there multiple heavens? Are we all God-breathed? If I die in this reality, will I see my Andrew again, or other-Nerissa's Andrew? And—

Dear Nerissa, you think too much. Yours truly, Gideon Selby.

The Doc decided turn about was fair play and was hovering over my shoulder as I wrote that bit, and stole the pen right out of my hand to scribble that note. Hey, you don't see me stealing your syringes because you take too much blood, Selby.

Later.

Tyler is some kind of engineering genius. This isn't only my opinion, either, Sapphira confirms it. I can't even explain what he did, but he set up some sort of relay where he pushed each probe further and further into the "weirdness" until they were strung out in a line, and now the one from the furthest point is transmitting information back along the line to the closest one, which in turn sends that to us.

Curiously enough, an hour or so after we got here, a strange probe popped out of the weirdness from the other side. You can imagine everyone's shock and excitement, and the reaction when our probes showed there was another *Caledonia* on the other side.

"Ah-ha!" Dr. Egghead stormed (supposedly; I suspect Tyler of slight exaggeration in the recounting of the tale). "I knew it! It's not a parallel universe at all. It's a mirror of sorts, set up to confuse us."

It does seem odd, having our counterpart ship hanging out there in our counterpart universe at the exact time we came back, but Tyler was able to do some readings on the other-probes, and they are real, not images of our probes reflected back, and the reports from our probes show enough tiny differences in the other-*Caledonia* to discount the Giant Space Mirror idea.

Then—and this is where things get really cool (or bizarre)—they figured out how to bounce communication along the string of probes, other-*Caledonia* using ours to communicate with us, our-*Caledonia* using theirs to respond.

According to Sapphira, who came to sickbay to fill Selby, Allain, me, and the rest of the staff in (we are all waiting with bated breath for new details as they emerge—Selby pretends to find our eager interest juvenile, but I haven't noticed him leaving whenever Sapphira, Tyler, or Chris come around with more info), the first conversation between the two was priceless. Something along the lines of:

The setting: The still-mysterious bridge of Our-Caledonia. A beeping from a com station. Captain Miles whirls, and sees his own face filling the main viewscreen.

Our Miles: Ha! Who are you, sir?

Other-Miles: Who are you, and what is this ... probe you seem to have sent to us out of nowhere?

Our-Miles: Answer my question, and I'll answer yours.

Other-Miles: I insist you answer me, and explain why you bear my face, before I say another word!

This goes on for a time, until both Sapphiras manage to persuade their captains to speak reasonably to each other, at which point the parallel universe fact is brought forth, and the two men manage to work together.

The other-*Caledonia* is also investigating the failed bio-freeze program, except they *only* have dead bodies, and there is no Riss-pod. I really did never make it to space in my own reality.

(I kind of want to thumb my nose at Dr. Egghead and say "Ha! Told you so," to Captain Miles over that, but I've decided that might be impolitic, not to mention immature.)

I'm not sure why they're still here, when we've been gone for three weeks—unless they also had continued on their journey and then had to turn back when AEF sent them a direct order. But why would Other-AEF do that without a Riss aboard to make it a priority? Or, I suppose, time might run different on the other side of the rift. Maybe they just barely arrived. Wouldn't that be a little too convenient, though?

I asked Tyler what he thinks, and he said that probably the rift warps time, and that whenever we came back to it, be it a day later or a month, it wouldn't matter, that even after we leave this part of space for good, there'll be a time-echo of both *Caledonias* left here for ages.

Now my head hurts.

The two Tylers have a theory about why the other side has dead bodies, and here there's me—and Sapphira just popped down to sickbay to tell me that since it directly affects me, they will allow me on the bridge as part of the meeting about this. Selby's coming too, since they might need his medical knowledge.

I get to see the bridge.

Later, Again.

I don't even know.

Saturday, May 15, 2016/Day Twenty-Six.

It was honestly pretty cool at first, going onto the bridge and looking at the other *Caledonia* on the big viewscreen. It was all ripply, with a rainbow of colors folded in layers over it, the result of the distortion between realities.

Then it switched to *their* bridge, and *their* Captain Miles started talking, his voice also distorted, but understandable.

Other-*Caledonia* had started looking into my history once they learned I was the touch point of the "X" of the realities intersecting.

They found that Nerissa Waldon, in their—my original—reality, never lost her husband. There was a car accident on her—my—road on April 23, 2015, but Andrew Waldon wasn't part of it. He and Nerissa lived—oh yes, there was no vanishing Riss from her couch a year after the accident—long and happy lives, had three kids (kids!), and died when they were very old, a few months apart from each other.

Captain Miles was, I think, at first inclined to veer over to Dr. Egghead's view of me when he heard that, but one look at my face convinced him this was as much news to me as it was to them. Selby had to catch me when the other-Miles told us about Andrew. It didn't feel so much like I got dizzy as that I was the only solid thing left in every galaxy, and the bridge, the ship, and space itself were whirling around me.

Even with Selby's support, I still staggered and went down to one knee, and stayed there for the rest of the conversation between ships.

So much for my excitement about getting to the bridge. I can barely remember now what it looked like, or who was there beside Captain Miles, Selby, and myself. I know in a vague way that the rest of the bridge crew was there, but Selby and Miles are the only faces I can see when I close my eyes and think back.

Tyler sent them the sample of my DNA from when I first arrived, and it matched theirs perfectly, so that confirmed that I was indeed from that reality. I wasn't paying him much attention, but I guess Dr. Egghead got pretty sour about that.

Time travel is pretty close to impossible to do *on purpose*, but with some engineering magic they managed to figure out how to have a conversation between times with little effort (something along the same principle as a phone call between the US and Australia in my time). I told them my cell phone number and they re-configured the com to be able to connect with such an old-fashioned device. Then they called other-Riss on the phone.

They recorded the conversation, and I've been listening to it over and over.

Other-Riss, answering her phone: Hello?

Other-Miles: Nerissa Waldon?

Other-Riss: Yes. Who is this?

Other-Miles: Ma'am, I have to ask if anything ... unusual has happened to you in the last few days.

Other-Riss: Who *is* this?

They go back and forth along this vein for a ridiculously long time.

Other-Riss: Look, just who are you, and can you explain what has happened to me?

Other-Miles, as persistent and implacable as this-Miles: So something unusual has happened.

Other-Riss: If you count going back in time and getting a second chance unusual, uh, yeah.

Other-Miles: Ms. Waldon, could you be more specific?

Other-Riss, obviously realizing she's not going to get anything more from this weirdo until she answers his questions: I signed up for the biochemical freezing space exploration program, went to the facility, entered the pod to be frozen, and then woke up next to my husband on the morning of his car accident. I thought it was a dream at first, but I wasn't going to take a chance. I pretended to be sick, so he called in to work and stayed home to take care of me. It's been a week now, and I haven't woken up, and I've just about decided it's not a dream, that I really did get a second chance with Andrew. Now, can *you* tell me how that happened and how you know about it, and who you are?

This-Riss (me), croakily, from the floor of the bridge with Selby bracing her and keeping her from utter collapse: Ask her what made her decide to do the freezing.

The question is relayed

Other-Riss: It was a stupid impulse. My sister called me on the night before the first anniversary of Andrew's death, and I felt so wretched and useless and miserable after I got done talking to her, that I called up the b o-freeze place at once and signed up for it. I thought I could maybe do something good in the future, and it would at least get me away from this life.

This-Riss: I didn't take the call.

[That was it. That was the one tiny thing that made two parallel-freaking universes connect for one moment of time. My choice to not talk to my sister that night. Even though normally one person's choice wouldn't make two universes touch like that. The Tylers discussed it while other-Miles updated other-Riss on everything, and they found that every other member of that expedition had decided to go in both realities.

They theorized that "the fabric of reality is thin" in this particular area of space. There are other known thin spots, so this isn't some bizarre, off-the-wall, spur-of-the-moment idea. Most are all really unstable, which is why people like Dr. Egghead believe there are no parallel universes, and the "thin" spots are pretty much the equivalent of black holes.

Anyway, they think that when the bio-freeze ship reached this thin spot, the difference between one missing (or added, depending on which universe you consider the "Prime" one) member caused a "ripple" in the fabric of reality and the parallel universes touched, and in the mess and confusion, the two Nerissas, being the catalyst for the parallel in the first place, accidentally got swapped.

She should have gone to that Wednesday before the first anniversary, though, the day we made the different decisions, so they're not exactly sure how she got sent back that extra year. I am choosing to call it a miracle, a gift from God or science or the universe, I don't care which. They're also not sure how I woke up, and didn't die, at just the right time, but again, I have to believe it is fate or God.]

This-Miles: So what do we do now? Can the two be switched back?

This-Tyler: Sir, we can't even get our ship any closer to the rift without it being destroyed. The probes will collapse on themselves in approximately fifteen minutes due to the distortion and pressure. There is no way to send Riss over.

Other-Tyler: And even if you could, I don't see how we could safely send her back in time, and bring this Nerissa Waldon forward, and then send her back to you.

This-Tyler: Whereupon we would have to try to send her back in time, which, again, we can't do safely.

This-Miles: So you are saying that both of them are stuck where they are.

Both Tylers: Yes, sir.

This-Tyler, apologetically, to me: Sorry, Riss.

After this was hashed out, and other-Riss learned that her counterpart was stuck in this reality, she asked if she could talk to me. The Captains, amazingly, agreed (apparently they do have hearts, just well-buried). The rest of the transcript is our conversation.

Other-Riss (Her): This is so weird.

This-Riss (Me): You're telling me.

Her: I'm so sorry.

Me: You saved Andrew's life in at least one reality. Don't be sorry.

Her: But it should be you.

Me: It's OK, really. If it wasn't you, it wouldn't have happened at all.

Her: Hey, you aren't fooling anybody here. I'm you, remember? Or you're me. Either way, I know you aren't OK.

Me: Right, fine. I'm ... I don't even know. It's horrible. But the part of me that's not screaming inside can recognize the truth of the matter. Which is that as much as I want to be there, I'd rather he be alive and with you than dead. I mean, it's not like he's with another woman, which would be even more bizarre and awful. He's still with me. Just ... not-me. Oh jeez, this is *so* weird. But I think, I think it's good.

Her: Not necessarily for you. I really am so sorry. But ...

Me: I know. You can't be that sorry, because you've got him again. And you shouldn't be. It's not like you did this on purpose. So just make the most of it, all right?

Her: Believe it. I won't squander this chance. I'll remember, every day.

Me: Good. Thanks. And I'll ... try to do something good here. I mean, there's got to be a reason I'm here and you're there, right? I'll try to figure it out and make it all worthwhile.

Tylers, in unison: The rift is getting unstable, sir. We're putting a lot of strain on it. There's only a few more minutes before it crushes the probes, and possibly collapses for good.

Other-Riss, to Other-Miles: Can I send a picture through my phone and have you get it to my counterpart?

Both Miles's: Yes.

And that was it. She sent the photo, other-Miles shot it through the rift, Tyler collected it, the rift collapsed (sending the ship spinning off into space, which I barely even noticed), and the two realities were sealed off from each other again.

I haven't even started processing.

Sapphira took charge of me after they got the *Caledonia* back under control. She got me to my quarters, where I tried to write and couldn't, and then she, Chris, and Tyler squished in somehow and sat with me all night. Tyler brought a bottle of really awful alien alcohol, and despite the fact that I'd avoided it after Andrew died, knowing he was alive but forever separated from me, without having a clue that his wife is really his other-wife was enough for me to accept the booze.

We all got tipsy, but not really drunk, and I think I was able to sleep for a little, I don't really remember. I don't think I said anything the entire time, and none of them tried to push, just were there with me.

They all left a little while ago, and Sapphira suggested I try to write through this. I haven't showered or eaten anything.

He's alive. O God, I can't get past that. He didn't die.

And I'm here, apart from him forever, and he doesn't even know.

He'll never know that he was supposed to die, and didn't, and that the wife with whom he had three children and lived a full and joyous life is from another reality.

Even the fact that I'm here forever pales beside that. My heart is torn between joy and anguish, and I just don't …

I've written, and I still can't

I just

It's so

There's someone at the door.

At least I'm not alone.

Part Two

Day Thirty/September 18, AY 102.

I'm not on Earth in the 21st century, and never will be again. Time to stop measuring time by their dates. It's Day Thirty of my new life, September 18th (it was April in my reality when I left, but August in this one when I arrived) of the Alliance Year 102 (I was surprised at first that they're still using Earth's Gregorian calendar to mark time, but the Arethran calendar is fluid due to the planet's erratic rotation, so when the Alliance began it was simpler to keep with Earth's major calendar, and so they have ever since). We passed Planet Hell for the second time yesterday, a sober day for everyone.

One month now I've been on this ship. The mind boggles.

I've asked for a meeting with Captain Miles today. I need to figure out something I can do on this ship for the next eight years. No more just putting one foot in front of the other. Time for an actual plan.

Granted, plans usually have a habit of turning upside down and going out the window as soon as you make them, but at least they're a place to start.

I have the picture that other-Riss sent hovering above my desk, a little miniature Andrew laughing at me with the sun in his eyes and his hair flopped across his forehead, sand stretching out behind him for miles, the sea just glinting in the background. I'm so thankful she sent it.

I'm so thankful *he lived*. It hurts like hell that he's not alive with me, but that he got to have the rest of his life at all is an amazing gift. I haven't had any nightmares at all since we learned everything, and if I ever do have any more, I don't think they'll be dead-Andrew nightmares.

That day—the day we made contact through the rift, and I talked to other-Riss, and we found out what had happened, and realized that I was here permanently, y'know, *that* day—is still surreal to me when I look back at it. I've honestly had to re-read that journal entry a few times a day, just to try to make it more clear to me.

The knock on the door that had ended the last entry was from, you guessed it, Selby.

"Please don't tell me I have to come back to sickbay, Selby," I pleaded with him as soon as I opened the door and saw his face.

He shook his head. "I think this situation qualifies for a house call instead," he said, so very gently that I knew I must be in worse shape than I even realized.

He waited patiently while I went into the head to change into my pajamas and brush my teeth, and then he tucked me in, handed me a mug of the inevitable chamomile tea, and sat beside me until I fell asleep.

Actually, beyond, because when I woke up in the middle of the night and wondered if it all had been another nightmare, I looked over and he was still there, sitting in my desk chair, sound asleep. Which made me realize, nope, not a nightmare, but also brought enough comfort that I was able to roll over and go back to sleep myself.

He'd left before I woke up the next morning. While I was still alone, I cleared the air with a good weep, and felt enough better after that to shower and dress. By the time an unnaturally subdued Chris came to check on me, I even felt like a human being. A weary, bewildered, emotionally bruised human being, I grant you, but a human being nonetheless. I made it through that day and the next, and by today feel ready to move forward, try to figure out what to do now that I'm here for good.

Everyone is still walking gently around me, except for Dr. Egghead, who clearly thinks this is all a plot to make him look bad, and is even more pissed because Mark Danvers thinks this is all wonderful and is writing his doctoral thesis on it and is probably going to be intergalactically famous for it.

Mark asked me to have supper with him last night to make sure I didn't mind him getting famous off my misadventure. I assured him that I was pleased to see anything beneficial that could come from any of this.

He was very excited, and very pleasant, and very handsome, and halfway through the dinner I realized he wanted it to be a date.

I freaked out a little inside, though I thankfully managed to stay calm on the surface. I wouldn't want to hurt his feelings. To his mind, despite the wedding ring I'm still wearing out of habit, all the events of the past month, especially the last few days, mean I'm an available woman. And I suppose, really, I am.

It's just, I don't think I'm ready to date. No, I *know* I'm not. It's too much—technically, Andrew's been dead for almost 500 years, along with other-Riss and everyone else from my life. And he was dead for a year of my life before other-Riss brought him back. Not to mention he's *with* other-Riss, not me. Or he was. Whatever. It's not like I'd be cheating on him, and yet ...

It's still weird. For me, I talked to other-Riss four days ago, and Andrew was alive again. But as soon as the phone call ended and the rift closed, that was it, end of story, they've been gone for 510 years. No more two-timelines-running-parallel-but-slightly-off.

At any rate, it'll be a long time before I'm ready to think about dating. I think I'm allowed to mourn my husband a while longer, no matter how bizarre the situation turned. Or at least mourn the situation itself.

I wasn't rude to Mark, but I kept it all fairly formal and polite. I think we parted on friendly terms, though not the more-than-friendly terms he'd wanted.

It was kind of a boost to even have someone interested in me at all, you know? Not like Mike, who proposed just because he thought he should take care of Andrew's wife. Mark didn't have any kind of ulterior motive like that, he was interested in me as me. And, I suppose, as a fascinating scientific phenomenon. But mostly me.

I may not be interested in dating yet, but it's nice to know there's somebody out there who'd be willing if I *was*.

Later.

No nightmare tonight, but I woke up abruptly from a sound sleep all the same. I lay in bed and stared out the porthole at the blackness punctuated with points of light for I don't know how long before I finally gave up on the thought of sleep, turned on the light, and grabbed the journal.

This is your new life, Nerissa.

Nope, still can't believe it.

I am aboard a spaceship, most specifically a *space corvette* (Captain Miles gets really annoyed if somebody calls it the wrong name). I am an unofficial member of the crew (or inconvenient baggage, depending on one's point of view) of an exploratory space-going vessel. I am 500 years out of place, in a universe not even my own, flying through space aboard a ship peopled with humans and aliens alike, out searching for brave new worlds.

How is this even possible?

A bit of "why me?" keeps trying to creep into my thinking, but I try to turn that into "why not me?" After all, for all I know, this sort of thing could happen frequently. Not with this specific universe, since they've never had it happen here before, but with others. Even if it doesn't, still, why shouldn't it happen to me? There's no particular reason why it happened to me and not to somebody else; it just did. I'm not some super-special being, nor should I be super-pitied.

I am, quite simply, Riss, in a bizarre adventure. And it's up to me to make it into a grand one.

Day Thirty-One/September 19, 102.

Captain Miles = big jerk. Have I mentioned that before?

He's a good Captain, I suppose. He cares about the people officially under his command. And he did find out what happened to me, for which I owe him. But he only did that because he was ordered to by AEF Command and he managed to make it work as part of his mission. Not because he was motivated by any compassion or concern for me.

At our meeting, I pointed out that I was going to be part of this ship's life until it returned to Earth, and I wanted to do something to contribute, so that I was not an unnecessary burden on the crew. I was going to ask what sort of civilian tasks there were I could help with—does the cook need help (answer: YES HE DOES THE FOOD IS TERRIBLE), does LS Petty Officer Parminetra need an assistant, or is there something simple I could be trained in, like directing mail or something, anything. At the very least, I could organize talent nights for entertainment.

He didn't give me a chance. Standing up from behind the desk (we were meeting in his briefing room, also called the star cabin, a small, cold room right off the bridge that acts as his office), he said,

"Ms. Waldon, the men and women aboard this ship have trained half their lives for the privilege of serving on this mission. Service aboard the *Caledonia* is not something you can just pick up on a whim. Every person here has a role, and every role is already filled. I agree that having you here is going to be a burden on the entire ship, but that is a burden we must bear as part of our duty. Good day."

And then he ushered me out and the door materialized behind me, firmly closed.

I was *so* pissed.

I don't care if Captain Miles is ex-navy, his unbending attitude is stupid. False, too. Look, just in the time since I've been here they've lost one crew member. So that's one spot at the least, and likely more (after all, my cabin belonged to someone who died before I got here, so there you go. Two spots, right there). Even if all the other crew members have shifted up a spot to fill their shoes, that leaves two spots at the bottom of the ladder, either of which I could be getting training to fill. Right? The Captain's just mad because I don't belong, and he's stuck with me, and so he's being a huge jerk about it. Which really sucks, because up until this, even though I didn't like him, I could at least respect him as a good captain. Now I can't ever do that anymore.

So I went to Engineering.

I'd been avoiding it because I knew Miles didn't want me in any vital areas, *trying* to be respectful. I was too mad to care about that anymore.

I've started figuring out my way around the ship. Occasionally I make it through two or even three junctions before I have to stop and tap for the map again. After only a few wrong turns and backtracking, I found myself outside engineering.

Chris's pal Ona, the one who did my hair, was coming out just as I reached the doorway. She's from Brazil, I think, and she has flowing black hair she keeps in a severe french braid when on duty and lets hang freely when off, enormous brown eyes in a heart-shaped face, and red, red, full lips. She's taller than both Chris and I, but not so tall as Sapphira, and very shy but sweet. She's Tyler's second-in-command in Engineering.

"Oh!" she said when she saw me.

"Hi, Ona," I said. "Thought I'd take Chief Tyler up on his offer to see what Engineering's like. Is he around?"

She obviously didn't think I ought to be there, but dealing with a shy person can have its advantages. She didn't want to directly kick me out, especially since I'd mentioned it was Tyler who'd invited me. So she took me to him in hopes that he would do the kicking out for her.

Alas for her hopes. His face came alive with delight when we rounded the corner to where he stood studying something at the big central console.

"Riss!" he said. "You ended up getting lost here after all!"

"This place is amazing," I said, looking around.

That was all the encouragement he needed. He relinquished his place at the console to Ona with a brief, "Keep an eye on those energy levels, I don't like the way they're fluctuating," and took me on a personalized tour of Engineering.

I was mostly struck by how clean it was. For some reason I'd been imagining it as a dark, greasy, smoky place, which was nonsense because this is a ship for sailing through space, not a 19th century coal burning steamboat. Everything was sparkling and orderly. Tyler hooked his arm through mine and pointed out all the places of interest—the engines themselves, of course; the transparent tubes running overhead; the wall panels showing all the different parts of the ship, so he can tell at a glance how each section is functioning; the various consoles which each perform a specific task ... it was overwhelming.

Tyler was supremely proud of it all. His crew worked away, barely taking any notice of their visitor, only their silent smiles or pink ears showing their pleasure when their boss raved about how amazing they all were at their jobs. Tyler seems the sort of fellow to inspire devoted loyalty in his staff, probably because he holds them to high standards and himself to an even higher, and lavishes praise when they live up to his expectations but never yells at them when they fail, just assures them they'll learn from their mistakes and do better next time.

One youngster was nearly in tears when we approached. His console wasn't working, and nothing he did made it any better.

"Did you try turning it off and turning it on again?" I asked.

Tyler laughed, and even the poor ensign managed a faint smile. "The more things change the more they stay the same," Tyler said. He gently moved the ensign aside to look at it himself.

"Hmm, hmm, hmm," he said. Then he pulled the front off the console and sprawled on the floor to look up at the insides.

"Here, Riss, good chance for you to see how these work," he said, so I got down beside him and dutifully stuck my head inside the console as well.

"See these threads?" he said, pointing to a humming network of impossibly thin blue, red, and yellow cables. "Best system in the world, but if they get knocked askew, the whole thing'll go out of whack. Let's see how clever you are, my girl. Can you see the ones that aren't working properly?"

"Uh ..." I squinted up at them, seeking some sort of clue. I didn't know anything about engineering, but it seemed unlikely Tyler would ask something of me that required specialized knowledge. Maybe if I thought of it more as a puzzle, looked for the pieces that didn't quite fit with the rest ...

Finally I pointed to two yellow threads. "I think those are supposed to be blue." Then I held my breath, hoping I hadn't made the stupidest mistake anyone had ever made aboard a spaceship.

Tyler laughed, but not in an "Oh my goodness this woman is an idiot" sort of way. More like in pleased surprise. "Brilliant!" he crowed. "Sometimes it's less about knowing the specs and more about learning the patterns. Here, wiggle out so Ensign Carr can see what went wrong and then he'll be able to fix it himself next time."

I obediently scooted out on my back, and looked up nto the faces of Captain Miles and Selby.

I was still grinning from having guessed the cables correctly, so I didn't panic over the thundering rage on the Captain's face as much as might have been sensible.

"Ah," I said, lightly smacking Tyler's boot. "Hello, Captain."

Tyler's head jerked up, smacking into the inside of the console. "Ow!"

His hands hooked up around the top and he pulled himself out. "A few more out of whack now," he grumbled, springing to his feet and offering me a hand up as well.

Captain Miles looked about ready to explode. Selby's face was sardonic as usual, but I thought I detected some amusement around the corners of his mouth.

Ensign Carr, answering a signal from Tyler, scuttled away as fast as he could go.

"What are you doing here?" Miles barked at me.

"Learning how a starship operates," I said brightly. "You wouldn't give me a job, so I have to find one myself."

"She's not too shabby," Tyler put in. "Got a good instinct for how things fit together."

I beamed at him. "Thank you." I turned back to the Captain. "My husband was an electrical engineer," I said. "You pick up a few things when you live with one for six years."

"Useful," he said. "A pity he's not here instead of you."

All amusement vanished from Selby's face, and Tyler sucked in an audible breath of air. My smile turned from real to fixed.

"Indeed," I said brittlely. "But since he was *dead* when I arrived, that wouldn't have been possible."

I was about to thank Tyler for the tour and hightail it out of there. Captain Miles opened his mouth to, I presume, order me out before I could leave of my own accord. Tyler's narrowed eyes and golden hue to his cheeks suggested he might have been about to break protocol and let the Captain have it.

Selby beat us all.

"Captain, I need a word," he snapped out. All of our spines straightened in response to that tone, even the Captain's.

"Doctor ..." Miles began.

"*Now*," said Selby.

He dragged him aside to a nearby console, while Tyler and I turned our backs and pretended we couldn't hear their very loud argument.

"You do *not* twit a woman about her dead husband, especially when she's just found out he's not dead but might as well be so far as she's concerned!" Selby said.

"Yeah," I muttered to Tyler. "Didn't they cover that specific situation in sensitivity training?"

He choked, trying to hold in a laugh. "I don't think the Captain attended any of those classes," he whispered back.

"I do not need this kind of nuisance aboard my ship!" Miles replied, sounding, I was glad to hear, somewhat subdued at the rebuke.

"Mm, definitely skipped sensitivity training," I said. "Also charm school."

"Then figure out a way for it to be not a nuisance," Selby said. "A good leader ought to be able to turn every situation to the ship's advantage. My last voyage, we were supposed to pick up a cargo of water, and ended up with watermelons instead. Did our Captain throw his hands up and moan about the situation? No, he ordered the cook to turn half the load into watermelon juice, and sold the rest for a profit."

"Doctor, I have no idea what you're ..."

Tyler buried his face on my shoulder to muffle his laughter. "The Doc and his stories

..." I made out.

"The point is, instead of asking Nerissa to stay in her cabin for the next eight years, study her talents and see how we can use them—and her—to the mission's best advantage! She's willing to pitch in, for Pete's sake. Would you turn away a willing volunteer, especially one who can't exactly go and offer her services elsewhere instead? Use your brain, man! Er—sir."

"People still say for Pete's sake in this century?" I asked.

Tyler's shoulders shook with laughter, and he didn't try to answer.

"What talents?" Captain Miles roared back, losing his temper for good. All around engineering, heads lifted as people stopped even pretending not to listen. I wasn't exactly thrilled to have my life discussed in so public a place, but hey, all my other really big private moments happen in front of others these days, why not this one? "She plays an antique instrument and sells outdated technology, Doctor. What could she possibly contribute to our mission?"

"He's got a point," I had to admit.

"Shush," Tyler said, lifting his head a little. "I don't believe a word of it."

"You're in charge, you figure it out!" Selby shouted, and with that, he stalked out, shaking his head and muttering imprecations under his breath.

"Chief Tyler!"

Tyler snapped to attention, spinning neatly on his heel to face the Captain. "Sir!"

"You, Commander Osei-Koné, and Dr. Selby are now in charge of Ms. Waldon's future role aboard this ship. Introduce her to new situations, observe, and report your findings and thoughts to me at the end of two weeks. Dismissed!"

I wasn't expecting an apology, but he could have at least acknowledged that I was still standing right there.

After Miles left, Tyler looked around Engineering. That's all, just looked, but every single member of the crew jumped and scurried back to their duties.

"Come on," he said to me. "You and Ensign Carr can fix the console."

Day Thirty-Two/September 20, 102.

Had a proper sit-down meeting with Sapphira, Tyler, and Selby this morning. In sickbay, naturally, where the majority of my life aboard this ship seems doomed to be spent.

(The real reason for this is because only the Captain has a proper office, and the mess isn't private enough, and personal cabins are generally too small for four people to sit comfortably, so sickbay it was.)

The only patient there was an unhappy ensign with a stomach bug—Merrill has recovered to the point where she can be back in her quarters, though she's still not cleared for duty—so Selby had Allain move the ensign to the far side of the room while we sat in and around his tiny office to talk in semi-privacy.

It was very much like a meeting with three college counselors. Selby sat behind his desk, Sapphira on one corner of it, and Tyler leaned up against the half-wall beside it, while I sat primly in a chair in front of the desk with my ankles crossed and my hands folded in my lap.

"So, Riss." Sapphira took charge of the conversation from the get-go. "What are some things you are interested in doing here on *Caledonia*, what do you see as your strengths and weaknesses, and is there anything you absolutely do not want to do?"

I had been expecting those sorts of questions, but when she fired them at me like that, I blanked (the same thing happened to me when I met with my high school advisor, my college counselor, and then my college advisor, as a matter of fact). "Uh ..." I said, with great eloquence.

The skin around Sapphira's eyes crinkled as she smiled. "Too much? All right, let's break it down a little."

Sometimes I think Sapphira forgets that not everyone thinks as quickly as she does.

"Is there anything you've seen since coming aboard *Caledonia* that's made you think, wow, I would really love to give that a try?"

I rested my elbow on the arm of the chair and settled one finger below my ear as I thought. "Honestly, I feel like everything that has happened hasn't given me the chance to think about things like that. It's been constant forward motion since I showed up here. I'm not complaining! It's made it easier for me to—" I almost said "assimilate," but that word has unfortunate sci-fi connotations for me— "adapt to my new, er, situation." And the time that wasn't spent in action I mostly used to try and wrap my head around the changes in my life.

"OK, so nothing on the ship itself has jumped up and down screaming 'Pick me,'" Tyler said. "Is there anything you think you'd be particularly good at?"

I spread my hands and shrugged my shoulders. "I don't know? It's hard to think of anything, honestly. I mean, not only am I completely untrained for this type of life, I'm also coming from 500 years in the past. I still need someone to explain the intricacies of my computer to me." I didn't tell them how bad I have always been with computers, and technology in general, even in my original time.

"Back on your Earth," Tyler began.

"Yes," I said.

"You were a musician."

"Yes. Which is completely different from musicians now," I hastily added.

"And you helped run a retail business?"

"Assistant manager of a used bookstore, yes," I answered.

"What sort of hobbies did you have? What did you like to do in your free time?"

Curling up with Andrew to watch old black-and-white movies (his favorite genre) didn't seem like the sort of answer they were looking for. "Well, reading. I mean, obviously, I worked in a used bookstore. But I was also part of a book club ... uh, I used to help out with church functions, nothing too important, just watched from behind the scenes to make sure everything was going smoothly, talked to people who seemed to be on the outskirts or uncomfortable, that sort of thing. My friend Sarah taught an art class, I used to go to that sometimes ... not that I ever wanted to be an artist, but I liked watching other people get excited when they were finally able to draw something they never thought they could, even if I couldn't draw anything myself. Um ..." I shrugged again. "I don't know. I tended to latch on to other people's hobbies more than develop many of my own."

Sapphira and Tyler looked at each other and did a sort of silent communication involving eyebrows and cheek scrunching. Selby just watched me with an unreadable expression on his face. I began to feel uncomfortably that I was revealing more about myself than I wanted.

"I'll tell you one area where I have thought I could help," I said brightly, drawing all their attention. "I'm not the world's greatest cook, but I'm pretty sure I could do a better job than—"

"No," said Sapphira, with a sigh.

"No," Tyler echoed mournfully.

"No," Selby said, speaking for the first time.

I raised my eyebrows at them all. "No?"

Sapphira: "Cook doesn't appreciate assistance."

Selby: "Cook was sent on this mission just to get him away from the rest of the Fleet for ten years."

Tyler: "Cook will chase anyone who suggests improvements to the food through the ship with a butcher knife."

"Ah." I revised my ideas. "Not cook's assistant, then."

"I think we're thinking too small," Tyler said. He spread his arms wide and lowered his voice to boom at me. "Riss! Tell us your dreams! If you could have anything in this universe, if you could *do* anything at all, unbound by *Caledonia* or the Fleet or even the Alliance itself ... what would it be?"

Go home to Andrew was my first thought, but I pushed it away. That wasn't an option.

Have Andrew join me here was my next, and it surprised me a little. Most of my imaginings had involved me magically switching places with other-Riss, waking up beside Andrew while she came here (after all, *she* was the one who wanted adventures in the future, not me), telling him all about the craziness of the last month and me slipping back into my old life, comfortable as my favorite sweatshirt which I'll never see again.

But having Andrew suddenly join me aboard *Caledonia* ... for a moment I lost my breath over how wonderful that would be. Because, truth to tell, I was starting to be sure I didn't want to go back, not now. Sure, I missed my friends, and even my family—despite our issues, we always loved each other—but I liked this life. It was exciting, and it gave me a chance to stretch my wings.

Then a bit of doubt trickled into my mind, sand through a crack. Would it be as wonderful as I thought, having Andrew here with me? Or would I fall back into his shadow?

This was the first time ever in my entire life that I was being taken for who I was, on my own merits, untinged by Andrew or Roz or Mira or my parents or my friends or my church. Just me. Just Riss.

It also meant that there was no one to cover for me or pick up the pieces when I let people down, but ...

It feels disloyal to write this. But it was honestly *exhilarating*, that for once it was just me. Would I have my friendships with the people here if I had shown up with an alive Andrew in the pod next to me? Would I have gone on the ground mission to Planet Hell, which, as horrible as that was, I wouldn't want to have not experienced (I mean, unless it could have not happened at all. But if it had to happen, I am thankful I was a part of it)? Would I have stood up to Selby way back in the beginning about my test results, and earned his respect?

All this passed through my mind while I recognized that I was really missing the point of what Tyler was trying to ask.

"I don't know," I said, quite honestly tired of saying that. "I think I would have to study up on what's even available to do here and now. I've been reading history like crazy ever since coming on board, but there's so much for me to catch up on. Technology, economy, diplomacy, biology, things I can't even think of! I need to absorb more of this universe before I can start dreaming of my place in it, I think."

Sapphira nodded in satisfaction, I think pleased that I was so sensible about it. Tyler, on the other hand, looked disappointed that he wasn't able to hand me my dream on a platter.

Selby, as usual, was impassive.

"Well," Sapphira said, standing up and brushing her hands against her pants, "What I think we'll do is have you try out different jobs, go about teaching you different things, until we find something that clicks for now. It doesn't have to be something formal, it doesn't have to set in motion what you are going to do with your life after we return from this mission, it doesn't even have to be the job you do for the rest of your time on the ship. But I am certain that, with the three of us observing, we'll be able to find something in the time frame the Captain's set."

"I'll put together a schedule and get each of us a copy," Tyler, the engineer with the orderly brain, said.

The two of them left, discussing what should happen when on the schedule. I stayed behind, mostly to ask Selby if there was anything else I could be doing for Merrill. Before I could form the question, though, he maneuvered his chair around the desk so he was facing me without any obstruction between us, and spoke first.

"Nerissa," Selby said, leaning forward and dangling his hands in front of his knees, "You know that you don't have to *do* anything to be ..." he paused, perhaps remembering our earlier conversation ... "valued. You're not—what's that old Earth story?—you're not Pinocchio, who needed to earn becoming a real boy. You are real. You are enough. Just as you are."

I closed my eyes against an emotion that was more pain than anything else. Oh, Selby was a good doctor, all right. He knew all about the importance of lancing a wound so the poison could come out and healing begin.

"Wanting something to do while aboard *Caledonia* is a great idea," he said. "Keeps you from getting bored, might even fill a need we didn't know we had before. Thinking about what you would do with your life if you were free from all practical considerations and restraints, that's good too. Good to stretch yourself, good to have dreams. But don't think that you need to do something to justify your existence. Just be. That's enough. It's more than enough."

My throat was too tight to answer that verbally. I nodded shortly and stood up. He followed suit.

"Let me guess," he said, lightening his tone to its usual sardonic vibe. "Now you're going to rush right back to your quarters and write down this scene as close to verbatim as you can get before it fades from memory."

His sarcasm enabled me to breathe again, and answer as casually. "Naturally," I said.

He rolled his eyes and pushed his hair back off his forehead, his sleeves falling back to reveal the black markings on his forearms. "If nothing else, we can always give you a role as mission archivist, recording everything that happens for posterity's sake."

I hesitated before heading out. "Is that actually a thing?"

"No," he retorted. "That's why they make things like reports, instead."

It was my turn to shrug. "Too bad."

That's actually a task I think I could perform—not only adequately—but with aplomb.

Day Thirty-Three/September 21, 102.

~~Space is empty, they say.~~

Space is cold, so I've always believed.
A black void (pit? bowl? something?)
Empty of compassion
Stranger to joy (ugh, crappy line)

Yet it is in space that I have found
The truest friendships
The deepest joy
The simplest faith.

To me, space is not cold. (this needs something) (like maybe a sledgehammer)
It is warm, it is glowing.
Sparks of light.
Dancing in the night.

Scrap it all, I think, except the last two lines.
Poetry is a lot harder when I can't fit the words to the melody in my head. I try humming it, but it's not the same.
Still, one must persevere.

We are all sparks of light
Dancing in the night
Shining with joy so bright
~~And my last line is trite.~~
Something-something-ight (white? Might? Fight? Sight? Ignite?)
~~Fading beyond my sight~~ (wait, when did this turn into a sad song?)

~~A beacon to ignite~~ (what does that even mean?)

Maybe the chorus only needs three lines? Can I adapt the melody to that? It feels unfinished. And I haven't even gotten to the verses, ugh.

Oh gee, look at the time. I'm supposed to meet Sapphira for my first task of the day. So long, crappy song that isn't capturing at all what I'm trying to say. Maybe you'll be more cooperative if I let you simmer in my brain for a while. Like, a year. Or ten.

Day Thirty-Five/September 23, 102.

Four days since the Captain and Selby's argument, and I'm afraid I'm proving Miles's point more than Selby's. Oh, I can figure out my way around any number of tasks if necessary, but there's absolutely no reason for me stumble around doing them when there are so many trained people here already whose whole *point* is to do those tasks.

Sapphira said "Hmm," when I told her that, and Tyler laughed and told me to go chat some more with Ensign Carr (who is a really sweet kid and terribly homesick, and does much better at his job after he's had a chance to chat to a sympathetic ear), and Selby said, "Don't be such an idiot."

So either they're all being very kind about my deficiencies, or they can see something I can't. Before coming here, I would've automatically assumed the former. Now, I'm slowly learning to not assume that I hold such little worth in other people's eyes. Or my own. I do know—it's taken me long enough, but I really do know—I have value, I'm just not certain how that value can be applied to this ship.

Instead of navel-gazing and fretting about it, I'm trusting my friends' instincts in this matter. In the meantime, I've been getting to know more of the people on the ship while I'm experimenting with different tasks, and learning about all the different species and cultures they represent.

Chris can't figure out why I'm so into learning about all this stuff. First of all, it's not like I grew up knowing about *any* alien cultures the way all of these people did. So I am way behind the grade curve here, and need to catch up. For example, nobody else expects Lieutenant Vreean to be at all interested in people, because her species only feel passion for numbers and patterns (which is what makes her such a spectacular navigator—that and the four arms, which allow her to input commands to the computer twice as fast as a two-armed being). But I didn't know that, and so I've been assuming she's just really snotty because she doesn't talk to anyone or eat any meals in the mess or even acknowledge that she has crewmates at all.

Which was a good reminder to me about people in general: don't make assumptions, Riss. Whether it be culture or history or species or the fact that someone stuck a stick up the Captain's rear, everyone's got their own story to tell.

Take Chris herself, as another example. She is Scandinavian (Sweden, Finland, and Norway have combined into one nation simply called Scandinavia), and couldn't understand why I found that so odd. "But ... you're *Asian*," I finally blurted. (Smooth, Riss. Zero points for cultural sensitivities.)

She looked blank. "My great-great grandparents emigrated from Thailand, sure. What's your point?"

I suppose if I identified myself as American to someone from pre-Pilgrim days, they'd wonder why I looked like a dumpy European instead of being tall and strong, with brown skin and black hair and eyes.

The second reason I'm looking up everything I can find about aliens is that it's *fascinating*. The similarities and differences with humanity, the little nuances and quirks ... I am beginning the understand the thrill of exploration everyone aboard this ship has, the joy of forging bonds with hitherto utterly unknown species, the amazement of discovering people and planets nobody else has ever seen before.

It's also, frankly, a lot easier to learn about various cultures and species when so many of them are right here for me to ask than it is for me to spend hours upon hours locked in my cabin looking up all the other information I'm behind on. And it's proving to be helpful in other ways, too: just the other day I got the Idiot's Guide to Alliance Economics from LSPO Parminetra when I was assisting her in the laundry. She's a treasure trove of information, and I got to learn all about currency, trade, production, the works. Stuff that I wouldn't even have thought of asking about, because while I slept through my college science classes, I didn't even *take* economics.

And not only was it surprisingly interesting, it gave me a clearer picture of the way this universe functions, and helped me feel a little less adrift.

Parminetra's people are mostly farmers—their entire moon is an agricultural dream, apparently, and they provide most of the off-planet food for Alliance consumption, making them one of the most important people. Because they are all farmers, though, they have historically been poor at defending themselves from invading species (of whom there are many, seeing what a useful place it is), so they exchange food for protection, and it's all very neat and tidy.

I couldn't tell you much about food production and exchange in my own time. I know that GMOs are supposed to be really bad or a natural part of your life, depending on who you ask, and that Big Corporations are destroying the American Farmer, or so everyone says. I always knew vaguely that I should care more about it, but never actually did anything beyond making sure that I always bought organic apples just to be on the safe side, and shopped at the local farmer's market whenever I could.

Talking to Parminetra about it, though, helped make the way the Alliance itself works more clear, and brought up a whole bunch of interesting side trails, like: Are all planets run by one government? And, Are each species known for One Big Thing, like farmers or navigators or being very logical, or does it tend to be more of a mixed bag? And, How did Parminetra end up aboard the *Caledonia* as a Logistics Specialist if her people are typically farmers?

I know it's not a strict ratio of one alien species to one planet. Tyler's home planet, Anah (which Roct, Parminetra's moon, orbits), has five separate sentient races who live in general harmony with each other. Other planets are similar; Earth and Arethra are kind of rare for each only having one sentient species. But how does that work out practically?

Seems like the more I learn, the more I realize is left for me to learn. I guess that's life, even when you aren't far from home.

I got an answer yesterday to one of the questions that's been bugging me since my arrival: who are the dominant species, and how do we decide when to use the "alien" label. Mark explained it to me over lunch. Each planet's species generally refers to all the rest as alien, and it's not an offensive term (whew). Humans and Arethrans are the most prevalent in the Alliance (Mark's grandmother is Arethran, and he showed me the black swirls on his arms, barely noticeable against his dark skin), but they are by no means the dominant species in the universe. Nobody is, so far as we know.

I also asked Mark why we don't have any proper diplomats on board. Tyler overheard the question and helped him answer. The Alliance is interested in exploration mostly for scientific reasons, to gain knowledge. Forming relationships with new species is secondary.

Literally. After our ship makes first contact with another species, and has formed the base for a relationship to be built, the Alliance will send an ambassadorial ship to start an embassy on that planet/moon/space station/etc, and they will start the more arduous process of forming proper diplomatic relations.

"OK," I said, processing this. "But what about first contact, how do you make sure that isn't an utter disaster?"

"We all have some basic diplomatic training," Tyler said. "It was part of the requirement to go on this mission."

"Even Captain Miles?" I asked. "And Dr. Eggleston?"

Mark snickered, and Tyler smirked.

"Some of us are better at it than others," Tyler said. "The Captain's handicapped by his naval background. Dr. Eggleston's ..."

"Just rude," Mark finished, leaning back in his seat.

I couldn't argue. I understand the reasoning behind the AEF's decision, but personally, I still think it's a mistake. Surely even for the sake of scientific knowledge, we ought to strive to learn all we can about other cultures, and to grow and broaden our own understanding with all this exploration. After all, aren't people—or peoples—more important than facts and figures?

I told Sapphira that at breakfast this morning, and she said "Hmm," again.

I am starting to sound like a broken record, but I so wish I had my guitar. Even a piano, or the fiddle, which I quit in college and never regretted until now. Heck, I'd settle for a harmonica. I'm starting to fill up with life again, and no place for it to spill over into. Poetry doesn't satisfy—some things are bigger than words. I need *music*.

Day Thirty-Six/September 24, 102.

Caledonia is a small ship, relatively speaking, with not much room. All the science equipment and laboratories have to go somewhere, of course, as well as storage of all our food, water, etc., not to mention the shuttles and engineering and sickbay and all the cabins and the weapons ... I get that there's not a lot of extra space one can utilize. But!

This ship seriously needs a lounge area, something besides just the mess. A place where people can just hang out and chat when they're off-duty, without having to feel like they must eat. There is the gymnasium (which is full of wicked cool futuristic machines for getting buff and some flight simulators, as well as the mats where Chris throws me around on a regular basis in my self-defense lessons), but people don't really go to the gym to chill.

The aeroponics lab is amazing and beautiful, but also not conducive to sitting and chatting. Too humid, for one. Too likely to be inhabited by the cook, for another.

No library, either. I suppose they aren't necessary in a world where all books are available through the computer, and nobody has hard copies of anything except as an oddity anymore. Still, it seems an unfriendly way of living to me, no libraries at all. Not to mention all the other stuff that librarians do—how can any kind of technology possibly replace a real live person for things like that? (Or anything, for that matter. No matter how cool technology is, people will always, always be more important.)

I took this journal down to the mess with me after I finished my last entry, hoping to be able to jot down some lyrics or possible melodies (though I really, really need to be able to pick out a melody as it comes to me—writing down the notes doesn't work for me until *after* I've already heard them).

Trying to reach one's muse in the midst of people busily eating—and the acoustics are lousy in there—is a dampening experience. I'm no hipster, to always have to work in *just the right* place, and I don't expect a coffee shop or open park here, but seriously. There has got to be some sort of happy medium.

I can recognize most of the crew by sight now, which is great, and of course they all know who the small, curly-purple-haired human woman in Chris's clothes is, even the ones I haven't met personally. I'd say I know about two-thirds of them by name, and many of them are becoming distinct personalities.

It is *good* to be able to feel an interest in people, and in life, again.

Back now from a brief chat with Ona and some of the other engineers who joined me at my table. They've all decided I'm OK because Tyler likes me, and because I rave so enthusiastically about Engineering in general. They were all pretty interested in hearing that I was trying to work on songs and not having any luck, and now they're all off at the other end of the table arguing over whether or not one could build a proper guitar from materials to be found aboard the *Caledonia*. I am starting to adore these people.

Ona told me that she used to play the drums at church when she was a teenager. I am so in love with the mental image of shy, efficient Ona rockin' it out with her church band, even though I know my image of what that looks like has got to be way different from the reality.

I want to talk to her about what religion in general is like now. I find it—I know I'm over-using this word—fascinating to think about. Is Christianity just for humans, or for all species? What sort of religions do alien cultures have? I am reminded of CS Lewis' space trilogy, where only the fallen peoples needed a Redeemer, but all peoples were created by God, which always seemed to me to be the most logical view, if one believed equally in alien species *and* a Creator God.

And what do Earth's religions look like now? How has Christianity itself evolved? I'll have to catch Ona alone to ask about this—I don't think she'll be comfortable talking that much about anything faith-related in front of her peers. The impression I've gathered in general is that atheism is the most prevalent belief system of the day.

I couldn't talk to God for so long after Andrew died. I am so grateful that no one in my church tried to force the issue, they gave me the space I needed to work through my anger and betrayal, and loved me when I couldn't sense God's love anymore. I had just started to come around when all this happened, and then I was too shocked by it all to even think about anything but what was happening.

Now, though, I'm finding myself thinking about God, and even talking to him again.

Part of me feels cheated—I had to go through all the pain of Andrew's death, and then that death was erased (but not the pain), but I don't get any of the benefit of his second life.

And yet, and yet. He *got* a second chance at life, and how could that have happened aside from God? And the very weirdness of all the events that have brought me here. I have to think that there is a hand behind it all, not forcing anyone into anything, but setting up events in such a way that we people have the chance to do something good, something we couldn't have done under different circumstances.

So I'm choosing to believe that God brought me here for a reason, rather than it all being a random sequence of mistakes, and that all the pain I endured from losing Andrew was not wasted. I'm a different Riss now than I was a year ago, that much is plain, and maybe I can do something here that nobody else could, and that I couldn't have done without going through that suffering. Maybe *that's* the answer to the "why me" that was troubling me right after everything with the other-*Caledonia*.

Or maybe it's that *I* get to be a better person here and now than I ever could have been before. It doesn't have to be some incredibly noble, highfalutin purpose that brought me here, after all.

Or maybe there's just one person that I can do good toward, that wouldn't have had that good otherwise. God cares for the infinitely small details as well as the grand.

In the end, I don't really care. I don't need to know. I only need to believe that at the end of the day, there was a reason behind it all, and that reason was for the good. That's enough for me.

(The argument about building me a guitar got really intense while I was writing that—half insisted you needed specific expertise in musical instruments to build a proper-sounding one, and half said they could figure it out with directions from the aether and what was the point of being an engineer if you couldn't design anything you wanted, and the first half rejoined that such an ancient instrument wouldn't be on the aether, and I finally broke it up by reminding them that you need *wood* for acoustic guitars, and since that is one thing we don't have much of aboard a starship, that put an end to the discussion. I am still so tickled that they even thought of doing that for me, though.)

Some of the engineers had to go back on duty, and they all slapped my back as they went and said, "See you around, Riss," or something along those lines. Even though I'm as out of place here as a palm tree in the middle of a pine forest, they still treat me as one of them.

It is, quite frankly, lovely.

I am intrigued by the instruments of this age. If we ever get back to Earth, I'd like to try my hand at a few of them. Not that I think I could ever produce music the way it is made now, but I'd like to see if I could incorporate my style of music with these new instruments. Who knows, maybe I could even start a folk revival. Wouldn't *that* be a grand way to leave my mark on this era!

Day Thirty-Seven/September 25, 102.

Surprised myself by bursting into tears while Ru El was trying to teach me how to fly a ship this morning (not, I hasten to add, on the actual bridge. He programmed the simulators in the gym to mimic the bridge's helm controls). He didn't do anything to cause it. He is dry and passionless, but not mean. He was explaining how the system works, and the next thing we both knew, I was sniffling and snuffling.

I thought I was adjusting well. Guess I had some emotions hidden away so tightly even I didn't know they were there.

My first instinct was to flee to my cabin and finish my cry in private. It didn't seem fair to Ru-El to do that, though, so I brought myself under control as best I could right there, while trying not to drip on the console.

"I am sorry," he said, hands fluttering helplessly. "I have said or done something amiss?"

"No," I said, drying my eyes on my sleeve and wishing I had a tissue at hand. No way was I going to wipe my nose on Chris's clothing, no matter how good the nano laundering system is aboard the ship. "No, Ru El. It's not you. I'm sorry. I have no idea what came over me." Sniff, sniff, try not to snort.

He patted my head. I think maybe he was aiming for my shoulder, but he's a little vague on human ideas of physical contact. Sapphira says it took them months to break him of the notion that all humans greeted each other with a kiss on the lips instead of a handshake. Someone in the Academy told him that as a joke, and it stuck.

Ru El's people don't go in much for humor—not as we understand humor, at least. I have, however, seen Ru El convulsed with laughter after pointing out the distance between two stars, so obviously they aren't completely humorless, just completely, well, alien.

(It's really mean to think this, but I would have loved to see the first time he met Captain Miles. Instead of a salute and handshake ... well, you get the picture. Captain Miles's *face*, can you imagine?)

"It is not an easy thing, finding one's place," he said. "Especially when one has had a place, and then that place isn't, anymore."

That's it exactly. My place that was now *isn't*, and I'm working so hard on finding my new place because I desperately want to belong, and not be a burden (and, OK, prove to Captain Miles that he was wrong about me). The pressure got to be too much.

I think it was the hopelessness of using the helm that broke me down. Ru El explained it all very well indeed, but none of it made any sense to me, which makes one more thing I can't do well.

Rather than dwelling on it, I finished off the lesson. Then I went to see if there was anyone else around who was maybe feeling miserable, on the principle that when you're unhappy, cheering someone else up is the best way to feel better yourself.

I came across Livruth, a fuzzy little white alien who is one of Chris's people and also from Anah, and who was nearly grey with homesickness. I had him tell me all about his home, and then I told him a little about mine, and then he took me to his cabin to show me some stills of his family ("stills" being this century's name for photos, which are three-dimensional and not really photos at all), and I think we both felt better when we parted.

It was better than running away to hide in the dark and hug my anguish tightly to my own chest.

But! Then!

(If this were a television series, or the "holo-tainment" Chris has told me about (oh my goodness, couldn't they come up with a better name than that?), I would cue the ominous music here, as our plucky heroine, displaced from her own life but courageously and cheerfully soldiering on, walks innocently down the corridor, unaware that DANGER LURKS around the next bend. **Dun dun dun**.)

In all fairness, I don't think Dr. Egghead was lurking. He looked just as startled and unhappy about our encounter as I felt when I rounded the corner and saw him there.

I would love to be able to report that he sneered and said: "So. It is you," or something else properly villain-like, but all he did was grunt. It was a scary grunt, though, okay?

I nodded and tried to edge past him without making it obvious I was running away.

I got by and was almost breathing again, when he said, "You!"

I thought about turning around and giving him big, innocent eyes and saying, "Who, me?" I didn't quite have the nerve to play that dumb. Instead I turned around and said, "Yes?"

He got really close to me then, narrowing his eyes and sticking his face right into mine. "I know who you really are," he said, his voice very, very quiet, and very, very terrifying. "Don't think you've fooled me. I'm watching you."

Then he stood up straight and backed away down the corridor, eyes never leaving mine, until he went around the corner and I couldn't see him any more.

Writing it down like this makes me feel like I'm making a mountain out of a molehill. At the moment, I was horribly frightened. I almost ran right to Sapphira or Selby to tell them about it, except I would have had to go in the same direction as Dr. Egghead to get to them and I was afraid he was still lurking. Instead I came here, and now that I've written it down, I don't think I need to bother them about it. So he's weird, and a little scary, and still thinks I'm some enemy in disguise. He didn't actually threaten me, and he didn't hurt me or even touch me, and I shouldn't need to go running to them every time I freak out over nothing.

I'll admit it: I don't want them to think I'm a coward. I also don't want to be a coward.

Dr. Eggleston is a respected scientist, and I can't imagine he'd have been allowed on a voyage like this if he had a history of violence. I'm still too used to being sheltered by my husband or my family, that's all. If he confronts me like that again, instead of standing there like an idiot, I'll calmly and firmly tell him that I have no vendetta against him or the ship, and that will be that.

It's really nothing to get so worked up over.

No big deal at all.

Day Thirty-Eight/ September 26, 102.

As I finished my shift in aeroponics today and headed toward the mess, a silver hand flashed out of one of the cargo bays and hauled me in. If I hadn't seen the color of the skin, I would have been seriously alarmed, thinking Dr. Egghead had moved from weird, non-threats to actual physical aggression. As it was, I was merely curious and a little annoyed.

"Jeez Tyler, did it occur to you to simply say, 'Hey Ross, come here?'" I grumbled, rubbing my arm.

He did not look repentant. "Shh," he hissed. "We're conspiring."

I raised my eyebrows. "What sort of conspiracy? And who is we?"

"Selby, me, Chris, Parminetra, and now you."

It couldn't be too dangerous of a conspiracy, in that case. Then again, it was Tyler.

"Sapphira's nameday is tomorrow," he said.

"What's a nameday?" I asked.

He stared at me. I stared back. "Don't you have namedays?"

I turned my open palm to face the ceiling. "If we did, do you think I'd be asking you about them?"

He tilted his head. "Fair point." He sat down on a barrel, crossed his legs, and rested his folded hands over one knee. "A nameday is a celebration of who you are. Humans and Arethrans place great store by names. A baby is not given his or her name until he or she is six weeks old, and then there is a big celebration, and every year after a person is honored on his or her nameday."

"Like a birthday," I said, curious as to when and how the change came about. Come to think of it, birthdays hadn't always been celebrated on Earth in one universal fashion, and I seemed to recall reading something about people who celebrated the birth date of their patron saint, instead of their own birth, which wasn't so different from a nameday. I supposed it was odder to think that there was now one set human/Arethran way of marking the passage of time in one's life than that they had changed from birthdays to namedays.

"I've heard of those," he said, looking pleased.

"Do your people have namedays?" I asked.

He shook his head. "We celebrate ... different types of markers. It's complicated."

As, apparently, were most things about his people.

"So, Sapphira's nameday," I prompted.

"Right!" Tyler sprang to his feet. "We are throwing her a party, but she doesn't know about it."

"How does she feel about surprises?" I asked.

"Hates 'em," he grinned. "But I think it would be more of a surprise to her at this point if we didn't throw her a party than if we did."

"So why are you keeping it a secret?" I paused, thought, and amended that to, "*How* are you keeping it a secret?"

He gave me a wounded look. "It's the fun of it, Riss! It's a game! Sapphira and I have been playing it since she was a new lieutenant fresh from the Academy and I a young—well, younger—petty officer, third class, both assigned to the same ship. I sneak around, trying to surprise her, she tries to figure it out—"

"And whichever of you succeeds, wins," I finished. Trust Tyler and Sapphira to turn a party into a competition.

"Selby is making the cake," he said. "Parminetra has snuck him some supplies she picked up at the last trading station from her own funds and has kept hidden ever since."

"Trading station?" I stopped before I could get distracted further. (*Note to self: ask someone later on about trading stations.*) "Selby is doing the baking?"

"Oh yeah, he likes to experiment with cooking and baking and the like," Tyler said casually. "He can't ever do it in the mess, because Cook, but we occasionally convert part of engineering into a rough kitchen for him. So, we're doing that, and Chris is in charge of inviting people at the last minute, so nobody can give it away."

"What do you need me for, then?" I asked. It sounded like they had it well in hand.

He looked around dramatically and hissed, "Distraction."

"Ah."

"She's good! Too good! If she comes near engineering while the Doc's making the cake, the whole thing is out in the open and we're sunk. As long as she's on duty, we're safe, but as soon as she's finished with her shift, we need you to distract her, keep her occupied for an hour or so. Otherwise she'll come prowling around, and she can see through all our diversions. Plus she outranks all of us so as a last resort she can always order us to tell the truth. You, on the other hand, are outside the chain of command." He grinned. "She can *try* to give you orders, but she can't throw you in the brig if you ignore them."

"Lovely," I said. In truth, I didn't mind. It sounded like fun, and as long as it wasn't going to really bother Sapphira, as long as both parties treated it as a game, I was in. "So when do you need me to waylay her?"

"About now," he said.

"Oh good, plenty of time to prepare," I said.

He grinned, stood up, and tugged my arm, drawing me out of the cargo bay and in the direction of the bridge. "You mean I'm not giving you any time to get stage fright. You'll be fine with improv, Riss! It's fun! Way better to think on your feet than to have the best plan in the universe."

That summed Tyler up, sure enough.

He dragged me off to lurk outside the bridge (sure hope Dr. Egghead wasn't watching me then, or his suspicions would have been confirmed) and then vanished, I assumed back toward Engineering. His timing was impeccable; no sooner had Tyler gone out of sight than Sapphira exited the bridge. She stopped short upon seeing me.

"Riss?" she said. "Everything all right?"

"Oh sure," I said. "I just—" and my mind blanked.

"Fun" to think on my feet, indeed!

A glimmer of understanding entered her eyes. She didn't quite smirk, but she came close. "Oh yes?" she asked, her voice unnaturally sweet. "You just what?"

Desperation aided my imagination. "I'm starting to freak out about never really belonging," I blurted.

It was effective, I will say. Sapphira lost all suspicions at once. "Oh, Riss," she said.

I began to babble. "I keep thinking that I'm never really going to fit in, that I'm always going to be scrambling to keep up, that I'll never have anything of value to offer all of you, despite—' But even for Tyler, I couldn't bring myself to tell her about Selby's telling me that I am enough, just as I am. "Despite how hard we're all trying," I finished.

We were walking down the corridor at this point, and I saw with dread that she was leading us toward Engineering.

"I really don't think it's anything to fret about, Riss," she said briskly. "You've already adapted amazingly well, and you've only been here a little over an Earth month. Give yourself time."

I cut her off before she could say anything else. "Where are we going?"

"I need to ask Chief Tyler something," she said, too casually.

"Oh," I said. "I don't think he's in Engineering right now."

She stopped. "It's his duty shift."

My mind raced, while her eyes narrowed and that almost-smirk appeared back on her face. "Uh, yeah. I saw him when I left aeroponics. He was in one of the cargo bays, I think, fixing something there or picking something up that they needed in Engineering, or—you know what? I don't really know, but it looked important."

She began walking again. "Well, I'm sure he's back in Engineering by now, and if not, we can wait there for him."

"Uh, could we not? I feel kind of awkward there right now, me being all emotional and stuff. I don't really want to talk to Tyler about this. I didn't even want to talk to you, but I know it's not good to hold everything inside, so ..."

She studied me carefully. "You don't want to go to Engineering."

"Um. No?"

"Even though they've practically adopted you and all think you're wonderful."

"Well, I don't want to ruin my good impression. You know, it's hard to think a person's wonderful when you see her blathering about how mixed-up and worried she is." I fixed her with a wide-eyed stare and blinked innocently.

"And you don't want to talk to Tyler, even though he treats you like a little sister."

"He's so confident all the time," I said with a shrug. "I don't think he'd get it." Then I paused. "You really think he thinks of me like a sister?"

"Why, you don't want him to think of you ... otherwise, do you?"

"No!" I practically shouted, turning bright red. This was distracting Sapphira from Engineering, certainly, but not in the manner I'd hoped.

I did not want to talk about *men* with her.

But apparently that was exactly what we were going to do.

She abandoned Engineering and took me back to her cabin, where she pushed me into a chair and sat down on a floating puffy cushion, pulling off her boots and tucking her feet underneath her. "Riss, do you have a crush on Tyler?"

"No," I said, more quietly but just as emphatically. "Honestly, I think of him as a brother. I didn't realize he felt the same about me. I thought he treated everyone the same."

"He is very generous in his affection," she agreed, still eying me with unnerving intensity. "But to anyone who knows him as well as I do, it's obvious you've won a special place in his heart."

"He probably gives stray kittens a home, too," I muttered.

Sapphira smiled politely at that, but made no response. Maybe they don't have stray cats in this century?

"I'm glad you don't have romantic feelings toward him, though," she said.

"Why?" I asked, genuinely curious.

"His people cannot liaison outside their own kind," she said.

"Cannot as in society forbids it, or cannot as in physically incapable?" I asked.

"The latter," she said. "And the former, actually. Even if he met someone compatible, he would not be able to form an attachment. He has been bonded since birth to his life partner."

"Oh," I said. "Wow."

Poor Ona. Her crush on Tyler was bound to go unrequited. The good thing was, she probably knew it. Likely I was the only one who didn't know this about Tyler's people.

"It's complex, and it's nothing like arranged marriages in Earth's old days," Sapphira continued. "Not oppressive, I mean. It—it's right. It fits. It works."

I took her word for it.

"Oh, and his people are born from eggs," she added. "Which the father carries."

She *almost* had me going on that, until I caught the twinkle in her eye. "That's not fair!" I protested, laughing. "I'm too easy a target for jokes like that."

"Sorry," she said, her beautiful laugh ringing around the small room. "I couldn't resist."

We continued to chat—not about men, to my relief, but about various alien customs and biologies—until I was certain Selby would have his cake finished and hidden. As I rose to leave, Sapphira asked,

"Better?"

I had to think for a moment. I'd almost forgotten my ostensible reason for waylaying her. "Oh—yeah," I said. "Thanks."

She just smiled again. "Any time."

Weirdly enough, I did feel better. Even though this had started as a ploy, it turned out to be balm to my spirit, as well.

It's nice having friends.

Day Thirty-Nine/September 27, 102.

I don't know why I even bothered getting a cabin on this ship. I spend most of my time in sickbay anyway.

I'm not sure which is worse, the reason I'm in here, or the fact that random members of the crew keep finding excuses to "drop by" so they can look at me and snigger.

Even Selby can't keep a straight face when he looks at me, and the whole thing is *his fault*.

"I didn't know the cake was going to make you turn green!" he protested when it first happened, while Tyler and Sapphira collapsed in a heap of giggles behind him. "Nothing like this has ever happened before with these ingredients! Nobody else was affected!"

Which would have been far more reassuring if his mouth hadn't been twitching in suppressed amusement the entire time.

Green. The first half of my piece of cake was fine. The flavor was unique, different from anything I'd ever tasted—a spiciness that had layers to it, with sweetness on the bottom, and I enjoyed trying to relate it to any of the spices with which I was familiar. Then, ever-so-slowly, I started to feel ill. Not in a horrible way, but my stomach started to churn a little.

Then Tyler looked at me and did a double-take. He grabbed Sapphira's arm, and she turned to look at me, and repeated his action. Naturally by this point I'm looking all around, wondering what they're staring at. Then Tyler started to guffaw, and a wave of laughter swept the room.

I grabbed Selby, who was closest. "What is going on?" I hissed, feeling utterly humiliated without having a clue why.

He stared too. "Oh damn," was his comment.

"What?" I said, and it was loud enough to cut through Sapphira's laughter.

"Oh Riss," she said. "Oh Riss, it's not you, it's just—well no, it is you, but it's not— Riss, look at your hands."

I did. Pale mint green, and darkening by the second. Oh, I'm a delight to see right now. It's even affected my hair, which is a greenish-brown shade to put Anne Shirley to shame.

"It must be because of the difference in genetic sequencing," Mark said, when he came to sickbay to consult with Selby. "It's not a normal allergic reaction. Something about the difference in her DNA must have interacted oddly with one of the ingredients. We'll have to do some testing."

"Oh, come on," I protested. "More testing, are you serious? You guys must have already tested me for every possible scenario in two universes."

Mark gestured at me. He, at least, had the decency to look at this as a fascinating scientific equation instead of the funniest joke all year. "Riss, you're green. Obviously we missed something."

I glared at them both. "I still think Selby slipped something in that cake on purpose."

"I wish I had," Selby said. "If only I were that clever. I think watching your skin slowly transform was the best nameday gift Sapphira's ever gotten."

I shot him a look of pure exasperation. "Thanks."

He grinned with the most open expression I had yet seen on his face. It startled me so much I couldn't think of anything else to say, and so sat there docilely while Allain apologetically drew my blood.

"You'll need to stay here overnight for observation," Selby said.

I sighed. "At this rate, I ought to bring my own linens for the bed."

He started to say something, looked at me, choked on a laugh, and wisely refrained from making any comment.

I'm sure if it weren't so humiliating, I'd find it hysterically funny myself. As it is, I would much rather lock myself up until I was back to normal, and never eat anything made by Selby again.

(OK. It's maybe a little funny. Maybe.)

I couldn't help myself. I started to snicker as I wrote the above, and before I knew it, I was howling with laughter myself. Selby looked over, saw that I was laughing and not crying, and joined in, followed by Allain and the rest of the sickbay crew, leaving only Mark, in the end, to stare at us bewilderedly and wonder what the joke was. Which only made us all laugh even harder. Naturally.

Day Forty/ September 28, 102.

I was attempting to teach Ona and Allain how to play poker (which would have been easier if my knowledge of the game was less fuzzy) when we were interrupted by a strange noise from Selby's office.

"What was that?" I asked.

Allain looked up from his cards (not cards really, just scraps of flimsy, bendable plastic-like material I inscribed with numbers and suits). "It's an Arethran word. It means basically, 'that's it,' or 'we found it' or ... you know. Like they used to say in your time, 'Eureka!' It's like that."

I decided not to tell him I had never heard anyone use the word "Eureka" un-ironically. "Ta-da," possibly. "Score" or "In your face" definitely, but not eureka.

"We've got it!" Mark said, popping around the half-wall with a beaming face. "We figured it out! The DNA in the *beletherin* spice reacted to the difference in your DNA and turned you green. There's nothing we can do to fix it, but the effect will wear off in a few days. You'll want to avoid that spice from now on, though, because with repeated exposure the green might become more ... er ... permanent."

"Um," I said. "Yeah. That would not be good."

"Be thankful it was no more serious," Selby said from behind Mark, his face settled back in its usual cranky lines. "Now that we know it's possible for your DNA to react with DNA of certain species in this universe, we'll have to be careful. Next time it might not be so harmless as a temporary skin discoloration."

I was about to dismiss his concerns with a scoff, until a horrible thought struck me. "Ona, Allain, can we pick this up again some other time?" I asked. They graciously left, and I went over to the office. I didn't mind Mark, but I preferred for this question to be asked in semi-privacy, at least.

"What, uh, what happens if I ever, well, uh, I mean, it's not likely but just in case, uh ..."

Selby folded his arms across his chest and waited. Mark stood by politely, waiting for me to spit it out.

"What if I ever get pregnant?" I blurted.

Selby unfolded his arms. He and Mark shared a glance.

"I hadn't thought of that," Mark admitted.

"Neither did I," Selby said.

They both turned that speculative glance on me. I sighed, knowing what was coming.

"More testing?"

"Actually, I'm not sure," Selby said. "There might be something ..."

"You think ...?" Mark asked.

"Maybe ..."

It was my turn to cross my arms. "You guys care to share with me, the patient?"

"We might be able to do an operation," Selby said at once. "To alter your DNA to match that of the people of this universe."

"Oh," I said.

After a few moments, I added, "Is it dangerous?"

They glanced at each other again, but, to give them due credit, neither hesitated in the slightest to give me the unvarnished truth.

"Yes," said Selby.

"A little," said Mark, more cautiously. "But," he added, "It might be more dangerous to leave your DNA unaltered. I mean, Dr. Selby is right. Anything you eat might set off a reaction, and one time it might be a permanent reaction, or a life-threatening one."

"The fact of the matter is, we don't know which is more dangerous," said Selby. "Up until just now, I had thought of it more as a joke than anything." He grimaced. "I don't know what your DNA would do if introduced into a new life form in this universe. It might not do anything. Your counterpart seemed to have been able to give birth without any problems whatsoever. On the other hand, this is 500 years later than your counterpart's life in your original universe, and you are getting exposed to all sorts of things she would not have experienced."

"I think we need to do more research before we make any decisions," Mark said.

"Yes," I said. "Research. That would be good. Thank you."

"We'll keep you informed of what we find, and in the end, the final choice will of course be yours," Selby said. "No one is going to force you to do anything, Nerissa. I give you my word on that."

He then discharged me, and I came back to my cabin to think.

Honestly, I'd thought of it as nothing more than a weird happening, par for the course with all the other weird things that have happened to me and around me since arriving. It hadn't even occurred to me that it might have more serious implications.

Of course I'll have the operation if Selby and Mark decide it's a better—and safer—option for me. Right? I would be stupid to not do it.

But, I don't know. It just seems weird. Like ... well, like changing my DNA would change me. Even though I know that doesn't make any scientific sense (but let's face it, none of this really makes sense to me), and that I'll be myself no matter what happens to me physically, it still would feel wrong.

Maybe I won't need to worry about it. Maybe they'll find that it's too dangerous, or unnecessary, to change me to match this universe. Maybe Selby will come up with some pill or something I can take every day to prevent my genes from reacting to anything in this universe.

I am going to be calm and sensible, and not worry about this until and unless it becomes relevant, and if that day comes, I will talk calmly and sensibly with Selby and Mark about my concerns and even the irrational fears, and we will all come up with a good plan of action.

Yes. That is what I am going to do.

Or, you know, I could lie awake all night for the next week fretting.

Day Forty-One/September 29, 102.

It's been ten days since the Captain challenged Sapphira, Selby, and Tyler to find me a position aboard *Caledonia*. Four days left, and then … well, I don't know what. If they haven't figured something out, will I have to spend the next eight years drifting around the ship like a lonely ghost? Or will eventually I find some sort of useful job to do without getting the Captain's permission? Should I be looking into some sort of education or career I can pursue from this far out? It takes a long time to get communications from Earth to us, and will only take longer the further out we get (talk about distance learning!). *Is* there anything I can do, this far from a university or any kind of businesses?

As if my newfound fear of my DNA wasn't enough for right now!

It's not all doom and gloom and me chewing my nails and fretting over my future. I use this journal as a way to pour out my fears so I don't have to burden others with them (yes, I know, Selby, I'm getting better about trusting others with myself, OK?), so its tone tends to be a little heavier than my days actually are. In fact, for the most part, life is really good right now. Surprisingly so, all things considered.

I feel more alive now than I ever did back on Earth—my Earth. It's almost like in the Narnia books, where the kids all become stronger, better versions of themselves under the influence of the Narnian air, and almost forget about their old life until they've returned to it. That's me. I've come through the wardrobe, and although *technically* the air of *Caledonia* is recycled and flat and not particularly inspiring, it's as though it is transforming me into a stronger, better Riss.

I'm *happy*. For the most part, I mean. I still have moments when I miss Andrew so much my stomach hurts, and I think murderous thoughts towards Other-Riss. I have times when I want to grab my phone and call Sarah, or invite Mike over for dinner. There are times when something strikes me as funny or poignant and I want so much to tell it to Roz and Mira, because no matter what else, we are sisters and in the end, nobody gets you like a sister. Sometimes I want a slice of pizza like nobody's business. I would pay a ridiculous amount of money for my clothes (and SHOES), my books, my guitar ... There are moments when looking out at the endlessness of space triggers my claustrophobia and I feel I must scream. Sometimes I long for a conversation in plain American English.

But those are just moments. Overall I am genuinely content and happy. And I think the total break from my old world has been good, coming away without anything but this journal (getting pretty close to full now) and my pajamas. It's good that everything, from food to language to people to environment, is so different. It makes it easier to fully live this life.

I keep thinking back to that conversation I had with Selby a few days ago, about not needing to justify my existence, and combining that with our conversation right after Planet Hell, about maybe it's okay to be a putterer. And how I need to place my value on who I *am*, not what I do. I think I'm finally starting to get a hold of that. It still slips out of my grip most of the time, but every once in a while I can settle on it.

Yes, it would be nicer to have a proper role in this new life, to feel like I'm actively contributing to *Caledonia*. But I've still got four days to figure out that role, and in the meantime—

Hang on. Someone's at the door.

Day Forty-Four/October 3, 102.

Only three days since my last entry? It feels like a lifetime.

No. That's an exaggeration. The first few months after Andrew's death (back when he was dead) felt like a lifetime. Were a lifetime, if you count lives by interior growth instead of years. This just feels like ... well, I'm not sure what. I'm still processing. Maybe if I start back at the beginning it will help straighten it all out for me.

So, the beginning:

The knock on my door at the end of my last entry turned out to be Dr. Egghead. I was, not unnaturally, surprised to see him, and a little apprehensive that he'd come to warn me of his scrutiny again.

I was even more surprised, therefore, when he forced a sickly smile and said, "Ms. Waldon. We've picked up an unknown object on our long-range sensors. The first mate wants you to observe, and has asked me to escort you to the bridge."

I knew my way to the bridge perfectly well by this point, though I hadn't been back there since the day we contacted the other-*Caledonia*, so I wasn't sure why Sapphira would want Egghead to take me there, but thought maybe she had noticed his increasing strangeness around me and wanted to improve our relations. At any rate, I said that would be fine, and followed him out.

I know it was stupid, OK? I didn't even need to have Sapphira, Chris, and Tyler all point that out to me, I figured it out for myself after about five minutes, when we were nowhere near the bridge, instead heading toward the back of the ship, the shuttle launch bay.

"Um, Dr. Eggleston?" I began, wishing I had thought to double-check with Sapphira before leaving my quarters, or that I was as capable of defending myself as Chris. "This, uh, isn't exactly the shortest way to the bridge."

He didn't say anything, and my nerves grew stronger. I stopped following. He went on a few paces, noticed I was no longer with him, and turned around and came back.

"You need to come with me," he said, no longer smiling.

I backed up a few paces. "Why?" I asked, in a brilliant attempt to stall while I tried to think of a way out of this. Unfortunately, we were in the middle of a long stretch of corridor with no branches or lifts, and naturally there was no crew around (I found out later Egghead had interfered with the duty roster in order to ensure that nobody saw us, but of course I didn't know that at the time).

He came up closer to me, and rather than flee, I decided to be brave and stand my ground, facing up to him instead of letting myself be cowed by a bully.

"If Captain Miles won't listen to me, I'll have to save the ship despite him," he said, his eyes glittering. He was so close I could see the sweat beading on his forehead. "You think I don't know about the ship?"

"What ship?" I asked. Yeah, add that one to the brilliant questions list.

He sneered, an expression I've always read about but never actually seen until then. "The mysterious 'unknown object' on our sensors, Ms. Waldon! It's your people. A ship, most likely, but I concede that it might be a traveling station."

"I honestly have no idea what you're talking about, Dr. Eggleston, but I'm going to leave now," I said, liking the way this was going less and less.

He grabbed my arm. "You aren't going anywhere except to the shuttles."

Nobody had ever grabbed me like that before. In a society and era where women are routinely cat-called, whistled at, and touched inappropriately, I had never experienced anything like that. I was always one of those who flew under the radar, attracting neither good nor bad attention.

I was so shocked I forgot all of Chris's lessons and merely tried to pull away. "Let go of me!" I said, my voice high and squeaky instead of the confident, commanding tone of Sapphira's I was trying to imitate.

We struggled for a few moments, and then he slapped the side of my neck with his free hand. It was such an odd move I didn't know what to make of it at first, until my vision started to cloud and my legs shook. Then I touched the spot on my neck and felt a raised bump.

"You …" I slurred, slumping down against the wall.

"A simple sedative," he said with satisfaction. He might have said more, but I blacked out then, and heard no more.

* * *

It could have been so much worse. He could have killed me then and there, or shoved me back in my bio-freeze casket, or dumped me into deep space, or anything. Instead, I woke up in one of the shuttles, with him at the helm. He hadn't bothered to tie me up or anything, just dumped me along one wall and left me there.

I lay for a few moments with my eyes closed, trying to calm my racing heart and still my thoughts. Panicking was the most attractive option, but didn't seem like it would get me far. I needed to be rational. I needed to be strong.

I needed to figure out what the heck Egghead was doing.

My long years of practicing self-control paid off here: even though I was terrified inside, I was able to be perfectly still physically. He didn't even know I was awake. I hoped to overhear him giving a nice villain-ish monologue, the kind that Reveals All and lets the hero know exactly what Must Be Done to Stop It.

Alas, he didn't even mutter, and I had serious doubts as to whether or not I was the hero of this story, anyway. That role would most likely go to Sapphira or Chris or whoever came out after us to rescue me.

I vowed that if I couldn't be the hero I would at least be the plucky sidekick instead of the damsel in distress (or worse, the character who is killed to increase dramatic tension and give the hero lots of angst).

Footsteps sounded, moving closer to me. I slitted my eyes to see Eggleston approaching.

"Should have worn off by now ..." he said.

He was strong, I had to remember that. But he wasn't expecting an attack, and I *had* been taking all those lessons from Chris. Besides, what other choice did I have? Other than to sit back and let him enact his dastardly plan, whatever that might be.

In other words, no choice at all.

He bent over me to check my condition, and I mustered all my courage and launched at him.

I hadn't taken into account that my limbs were cramped and prickly from being in one position for so long. My launch turned into a lurch, but thankfully Egghead was so surprised that I still managed to knock him down.

For a moment, I felt a surge of triumph, but he recovered from his surprise quickly, and then the real struggle began. He was strong despite his white hair, and had the passion of his beliefs behind him. On the other hand, I was young, at least a little bit trained, and fighting for my life and out of terror. We were evenly matched.

Back and forth across the shuttle we surged, wrestling and throwing punches and using every trick we had to gain an advantage over the other. I was briefly distracted by wondering who was flying the shuttle while we fought, but then remembered Ru El's lectures, and that the shuttles could be put on autopilot in deep space; the proximity alarm would sound if they neared anything that required sentient maneuvers.

Dr. Egghead took advantage of my distraction to land a punch squarely in my stomach. While I bent over, wheezing, he followed that up with a one-two combination to the sides of my head. I slumped forward, catching myself with my hands on the floor.

"Ha!" said Egghead.

He was sure he had won. At first, I thought so, too. I closed my eyes, and let the old, familiar feelings of uselessness and inadequacy wash over me. Wasn't smart enough to know that Eggleston was plotting against me; too much bravado to run when I had the chance; not strong enough to fight him off now.

A fire flared in my heart. No, I was *not* useless. Maybe I'd gotten myself in a bad situation, but after all that I'd done and learned, I was not going to let that define me. I was going to get myself out of this!

I pushed back up, once again taking Egghead by surprise. He was still busy gloating, and didn't have a chance to defend himself. I tossed Chris's teaching aside and reverted to the football games we used to play in the backyard, Mike and Tom and me against Sarah and Andrew and Megan. We all cheated horribly, and nobody cared in the slightest about the score, but I had learned a few dirty moves. I tackled Eggleston low and knocked him flat on his back.

He stared up at me in shock before I grabbed his head and banged it against the floor a few times, stopping only when his eyes rolled up in the back of his head and I was certain he was unconscious.

Then I scrambled backward and tried not to throw up at what I'd just done. I'd never deliberately used violence against another individual before, never tried to harm someone. It was ... unnerving.

Finally I got the shaking under control enough to think about my next move. Obviously I didn't want to leave Eggleston (somehow it was harder to think of him as Dr. Egghead after smashing his head against the metal floor of the shuttle) free to wake up and start the fight all over again. I did some hunting around and found some zip tie-like things in the repair kit, which I used to secure his wrists and ankles.

Then I checked his pulse to make sure I hadn't killed him. It was still strong, which brought a gush of relief to my heart, and freed me to think less about him and more about *what next*.

Ru El had taught me how to use communications. As delightful as it would have been to arrive back at *Caledonia* on my own, triumphantly flying the shuttle with my prisoner secured, the day saved and the ship not having to go out of her way in the slightest, that was not practical. I had no idea where we were, much less where we were in relation to *Caledonia*, and while I had learned the rudiments of how to fly, I was not good enough to get anywhere even if I knew where to go.

I slid into the pilot's chair, still shaking, and set the comm panel to "distress call." That would send out a notification to any ships in the area that there was someone in, well, distress, here.

"My name is Nerissa Waldon, currently with the AEF ship *Caledonia* under the command of Captain Miles," I said, then paused. What to add next? "I was kidnapped but am fine now" seemed a little ingenuous. Besides, it didn't seem right to give too much detail. It was a signal for help, not a dissertation. Best just to state my needs. "I have a prisoner and am in need of assistance returning to my ship."

I hit "send." The message would broadcast from the shuttle over and over again until I stopped it or someone came.

The next several hours were dreadful. I found the emergency supplies and drank a little water, ate half a ration bar. Without knowing how long we'd be out here, I didn't want to take too much. I paced back and forth and tried to figure out how to read the displays telling us where we were. Eggleston woke up, and spewed vituperation at me until I gagged him with a strip torn from his own coat. I found the medical kit and cleaned myself up as best I could. I paced some more.

For the most part, I just waited, slumped in the pilot's chair with Eggleston staring hatred into my back.

It finally occurred to me that he could die from dehydration, so I walked over and removed the gag. His eyes were bloodshot and filled with rage, but he didn't say anything. I held the water tube to his lips and let him take a few swallows. When I pulled it back, he licked his lips and spoke one word.

"More."

His voice was hoarse, but still imperious. I shook my head.

"Torture?" It was amazing how he could sneer while bloodied and bound on a cold metal floor.

I scooted back and sat down, resting my back against the shuttle's wall. As irritating as the man was, any conversation was better than the black silence of space and his hatred. "Don't be ridiculous." I tried to make my voice as crisp and professional as Sapphira's. "But I don't know how long we'll be out here, and I don't want to waste our resources. You're the one who planned this kidnapping; if you'd wanted more water, you should have packed it."

"I suppose I should have expected treachery from you," he said.

"Treachery?" It was no good; I couldn't be Sapphira. My voice went high and squeaky on that word, and I lost all pretense of coolness. "You lure me into a deserted part of the ship, drug me, drag me onto this shuttle and fly me out into who-knows-where, and when I defend myself against you, you call it treachery?"

He was silent. After a little, I couldn't help myself.

"What was your plan, anyway?"

"As if I would tell it to you!" he spat.

I gestured at our surroundings. "Oh, come off your high horse, Egghead. Look around. You can't still seriously believe I'm some super-duper spy, can you? If I were, don't you think I'd be managing things a bit better by now?"

His eyes bulged from his head in outrage. "*What* did you call me?"

Oops. I hadn't meant to let that sobriquet slip. I hurried on without answering the question. "Would I really have fallen for your ploy, if I were a spy? Wouldn't I be more suspicious? And don't you think I'd have had an easier time subduing you? And would I still be sitting here, twiddling my thumbs, waiting for *Caledonia* to find us, if I had another option?"

He didn't say anything for a few moments. Then,

"I admit, you are far more ... inadequate at your job than I was expecting. You were obviously chosen for your role due to your skill at deception, rather than planning or self-defense."

"Thanks," I said. "Look, tell me this: why are you so absolutely certain that I must be a spy and an enemy, instead of what I claim to be?"

He tried to sit up, he was so outraged at the question. Deciding to show a little basic compassion, I went over to him and helped prop him into a sitting position against the wall, a mimic of the pose I now resumed.

I didn't expect any thanks, nor did I receive any.

"There is no such thing as a parallel universe! A person cannot travel through time! They are scientific impossibilities! Your claims cannot be true, so you must be lying, and the only reason for you to lie is if you wish us ill."

I grabbed my hair, and was briefly startled by the sight of my still-green hands. The hue was fading, but not gone entirely. Sapphira's party seemed worlds away. "But you were there, on the bridge, when we broke through the barrier between universes, and spoke to the other-*Caledonia*. How can you deny something you saw with your own eyes?"

"It was a trick," he insisted, though he looked a little desperate by now. "It must have been. It is a scientific impossibility for a parallel universe to exist."

Sitting there, looking at him, something clicked for me. He wasn't just a stubborn, crazed old man. He was a religious fanatic. Science was his religion, and just as certain members of various religions through the ages would deny the evidence of their senses if it contradicted their beliefs, so he had to do when something went against his scientific beliefs. For the first time, I felt a stirring of pity.

"I don't pretend to understand much about science," I said. "I have to say that all this seems pretty impossible to me. I mean, in my day, nobody even believed faster-than-light travel was possible, or that humans and other species could co-exist in the same environment. Oh, it's popular enough in science-fiction, but everybody *knows* it could never happen in real life. Yet here I am, and here all you are."

I took a deep breath. Eggleston, for once, didn't interrupt. "And long before my time, they called Galileo a heretic for believing the sun was the center of the universe. Isn't it possible that there are truths out there beyond the reach of science-as-you-know-it? That your science is, perhaps, not infallible?"

He sniffed with superb disdain. "No."

So much for that line of reasoning.

I rubbed my nose. "OK. So there's no way I could actually have come from the past or from a parallel universe, or both. Right?"

He sniffed again. I took that as assent.

"Is it at all possible that there's another option besides me being evil? I mean … could I have been kidnapped by these enemies you claim are out to get you and *Caledonia*, and brainwashed into believing all that stuff about my former life?"

There was a long pause, but he did not sniff, which I thought encouraging. Finally, he said, "It is far-fetched, but I suppose barely possible."

"Improbable but not impossible," I said. "Great. Now we're getting somewhere. Any other options?"

"Why search for other options when the obvious one is almost always the most likely?" he inquired.

One step forward, two steps back. "Almost always," I stressed. "Not inevitable. Besides, maybe it just seems like the most obvious. Maybe—" I had a flash of inspiration. "—Maybe that's what we're *supposed* to think. Maybe it really is a plot, and we're all victims, me included."

He looked skeptical, but for the first time, his eyes actually focused on *me*, not on the person he thought he saw whenever he looked at me.

I hurried to take advantage of this. "So, what are some of the other options. If we start with the premise that there cannot be a parallel universe or time travel *and* that I am innocent of any wrong-doing, what are some possible explanations?"

"I ... do not know," he said.

I stood up. "Well, you're the expert in hypotheses. I'll leave you to think about it while I try to figure out why *Caledonia* hasn't responded to our distress call yet. I was sure they would hear it."

"Oh, I turned off the receiver," said Eggleston indifferently, already chewing over this new problem. "You can't receive any incoming transmissions until you turn it back on. I didn't want to be distracted while taking you back to your people."

"Oh!" I exclaimed, leaping for the console. Then I stopped and turned back. "Wait, *what*?"

"Hadn't you figured that out? I was taking the shuttle to meet the unknown ship ahead of *Caledonia*, and I planned to threaten to kill you if they didn't leave us alone."

"You were going to kill me?"

I could think of any number of problems with his plan, the first being that he had absolutely no proof whatsoever the unknown object on *Caledonia's* long-range sensors even was a ship. Of more immediate concern to me was that even if it was a ship, it wasn't "my people," and so he would have ...

Righteous indignation stamped itself all over his features. "Of course not! I am not a murderer, no matter how vile you and your people might be."

That was mildly reassuring. He'd drug and kidnap me, but he hadn't actually intended to harm me. Until I attacked him, that is. Darn it. I couldn't help but feel a modicum of respect along with my fear, anger, and mild guilt. He was a slimy weasel who didn't care about the people under his command, but he cared enough about the ship and the sanctity of the mission that he was willing to put himself in danger to protect both, and to attempt to do so without taking my life.

I put the matter out of my head temporarily, examined the console, brought to mind my lessons from Ru El, and pressed the button I thought would allow me to receive outside messages.

Instantly, the shuttle filled with the mellifluous, annoyed tones of Captain Miles. "—ease respond. Repeat. Ms. Waldon and Dr. Eggleston, if you can hear this, please respond. Repeat, Ms. Waldon—"

I started shaking again. I never thought I'd be so happy to hear that voice. It took me two tries, because I was so overwrought, but finally I managed to hit the button that would kill the distress call and allow me to respond directly to *Caledonia*.

"Yes! Yes, this is Riss. I'm here. I'm here. Where are you?"

The recorded message broke off. "Ms. Waldon?" said the Captain.

Who else would it be? "Yes," I said, trying to calm down. "This is Nerissa Waldon. I'm in the shuttle. Dr. Eggleston is, er, here as well."

"Where is 'here,' exactly? We have been sweeping space with our sensors ever since we heard the distress call, but we have not been able to pinpoint your location."

Eggleston spoke up behind me, sounding insufferably smug. "I changed our hull resonance to dissipate sensors and scatter them. We are, practically speaking, invisible."

"What?" Miles sounded startled. "Eggleston, is that you? What did you say? Why did you—Never mind. Just tell me your location."

"Uh, it's, uh ..." I scanned the console frantically. "Remind me again where I would find that?"

The Captain's silence was eloquent.

"Left hand side, upper corner, Riss," came Ru El's voice. "Ask Dr. Eggleston to show you. He knows."

"He's, uh, a little tied up at the moment," I said, and then had to hold back an entirely inappropriate snicker even as said doctor sniffed in outrage behind me. "Found them! Thanks, Ru El." I rattled off the stream of numbers that meant nothing to me, but apparently told something to *Caledonia*.

"We are on our way to you," said the Captain. "But it would help if you could also come toward our coordinates."

Right, meet in the middle, save some time. "Sure," I said. "I just put your coordinates into the little blinky box in the middle of the console, hit enter, and the shuttle goes toward them, right?"

"Inelegant, but adequate," Captain Miles said dryly.

Ru El read me their coordinates, I input them, and I felt the shuttle vibrate to life underneath me.

At last, something was happening.

Of course, it didn't exactly end like that. It was another several hours before I finally saw *Caledonia* looming through my viewscreen. Sleek and shining silver, it already looked like home to me. I honestly felt a lump in my throat at the sight of it.

Then a warning siren went off.

"You have to stop the shuttle, you idiot," Eggleston hissed behind me. "It's still moving toward where *Caledonia* was before coming to meet us; if you don't kill the acceleration we'll crash!"

Oops. I remembered how to make an emergency stop, right enough. I hit the console, and we shuddered to a halt. Eggleston breathed a sigh of relief.

"Thanks," I tossed over my shoulder.

"I didn't mind dying when it would have proved me right, but I object to getting squashed on the bow of my own ship because some stupid girl forgot to put on the brakes," he snapped.

"Thanks anyway," I shot back, sick and tired of his attitude.

A small beep and flashing light let me know *Caledonia* wanted to talk again.

"Yes, go ahead," I said.

"Riss, this is Sapphira," she said, and again that lump rose in my throat. "We can see you, but we still aren't picking you up on our sensors. You're going to have to maneuver the shuttle into the bay yourself."

"What?" I squeaked. I spun around to glare at Eggleston. "Tell me how to turn off that field-thing that's messing with their sensors!"

"It's not a button you can push, girl," he barked back. "It was a complicated and delicate process, and involved installing deflectors on the outside of the shuttle. Unless you want to suit up and crawl around the hull …?"

I stared at him for a few moments in pure, impotent fury, then whirled back to face the console.

"Riss, you still there?"

I pushed my hair back with both hands. "Yeah. Yeah, Sapphira, I'm here."

"If we can't pick you up on sensors, we can't lock onto you and drag you into the bay with grapple beam. So you're going to have to do it. Ru El will talk you through it. We've cleared one of the bays out entirely, so even if it's a little messy, you aren't likely to do much damage."

"Except maybe to us," Eggleston interjected sarcastically. "Listen, girl, untie me. I can fly us back in."

"Ha!" I said. "Not likely. You'll turn around and whisk us off into deep space again. I really would be the idiot you call me if I did that."

"Not at all." He smiled. It looked painful. "I've been thinking about what you said, and I agree that perhaps there is another explanation to your presence. I'm willing to input some possibilities into a program on my computer, work out the odds, come up with a hypothesis. You needn't fear me, er, Nerissa."

I hesitated.

"It's your choice, Riss," said Sapphira. "Trust Dr. Eggleston to bring you back, or do it yourself."

I sighed. "Ru El, what do I need to do first?"

The next half hour was torture, with Egghead's unhelpful interjections distracting me from Ru El's calm, steady directions, my heart in my mouth and every moment certain we were going to crash against the side of the ship, but eventually I brought us in, and I only scraped the side of the bay door a *little*. I don't care what Egghead says.

It was uncannily like my first arrival on the ship, with the entire senior staff awaiting us when we exited the shuttle. I'd taken the ankle ties off Egghead so he could walk, but kept his wrists bound and made him walk in front of me.

The Captain kept his impassive expression, but I could see shock and horror on Chris' face, and sheer fury as she took Eggleston into custody. Sapphira seemed torn between pride and anger, Tyler gingerly patted my shoulder silently, and Selby, looking angrier than I've ever seen him, ordered me to sickbay without any extraneous words. He kept me there until this morning, no journal allowed, although he's hardly spoken to me at all, and Allain did all my treatment.

Wow, just writing all that out took all the energy I've got. Time for a nap now, I think. See, Selby? I can be sensible sometimes.

Day Forty-Six/October 5, 102.

I got mad today and stormed down to sickbay. Allain and the rest of the people on duty saw me come in and scattered for cover. I marched up to Selby's desk and glared down my nose at him.

"I thought we were friends," I snapped.

He raised his eyebrows. "Good morning?" he suggested.

"Not particularly," I replied. I drew a deep breath. "Look, I realize that I was all kinds of stupid in letting Dr. Eggleston trick me. I also realize that as a doctor and, well, person of any kind of compassion, you were horrified at what I did to him in order to escape, especially when he didn't intend any real harm to me at all, just wanted to get me off the ship. But for crying out loud, yell at me for it, tell me how you feel, get it out of your system, so that we can move on. Don't sit in here sulking about it and refusing to talk to me. You're acting like a three-year-old. This is not the Gideon Selby I thought I could trust with—with absolutely anything."

He didn't say anything for a few moments, just long enough for me to start to feel like an idiot. Then he came to his feet with one abrupt movement.

"Allain, I'm taking a break," he called.

Allain cautiously poked his head out of whatever hole he had hidden in, saw that we didn't look entirely ready to kill each other or anyone else, and emerged. "You got it, boss," he said, then gave me an encouraging smile behind Selby's back.

I like Allain.

"Will you walk with me, Nerissa?" Selby asked.

I nodded, and we stepped out of sickbay to pace through the corridors in relative privacy.

"You're right," he said, as he had done before when I confronted him. "And you're wrong." He stared straight ahead. "Nerissa, I—I don't—" He stopped, then tried again. "I don't think you quite understand what it was like for us here, when you and Eggleston vanished like that, without a trace."

"I'm sure Captain Miles was pissed," I said.

Selby gave half a smile. "True. But underneath that, you could tell he was genuinely worried. Chris blamed herself, you know. As head of security, she felt it was her fault that Eggleston was able to whisk you off like that."

So she'd told me, after she finished yelling at me for everything I did wrong, starting with not running away as soon as my instincts told me something was off. ("Running away is always the first and best plan, Riss!" she sputtered. "Don't you know anything? It's not cowardice, it's common sense!" I know it *now*, Chris.)

"How did you all know it was Eggleston who took me?" I inquired, breaking into his story. Nobody had told me anything useful, really, since my return.

He gave me a look. "We were fairly certain you two weren't eloping."

I snorted.

"We didn't know what had happened, but we knew you wouldn't have left the ship voluntarily without telling someone. Danvers told us that Eggleston's behavior has become increasingly erratic in the last few weeks—it wasn't hard to figure out that he had taken you for some reason, though I don't think any of us knew just how paranoid he had really become about you." He swallowed. "So, there you were, gone, and that was bad enough. But then we couldn't find the shuttle anywhere. No trace, no hint, nothing. It was as if you had been swallowed by space. And we—and I—" He stopped again.

"I'm sorry," I said softly. I could only imagine how frantic they must have been.

He held up his hand to stop me from saying anything more. "Don't. Don't apologize. Please, Nerissa."

"O…K?" I said hesitantly.

He continued. "Then we finally made contact with you, and you sounded fine but I knew something was wrong, I could tell by your voice, and then … then, Nerissa, when you actually landed that damn shuttle and stepped off of it, with Eggleston as your prisoner and you so badly beaten, obviously by him, and seeing the evidence of what you had to do to him …" He stopped again, started again. This was the most visibly distressed I'd ever seen Selby. I didn't like it, not one bit. I wanted the old, sardonic Selby back.

This was better than the silent, refusing-to-acknowledge-my-existence Selby, though, so I let him continue.

"I was furious," he said bluntly.

"No joke," I murmured.

"Not at you, though." This time, he stopped walking as well as talking, and turned to face me, reaching out to cup my chin in his hand. "Damn it, Nerissa, how can you think that? How could I be angry at you?"

"Because I was an idiot who let myself get kidnapped, and then resorted to violence to free myself?" I suggested, finding myself just slightly out of breath.

He dropped his hand and stepped back. "The idiot thing I grant you, but even so, Nerissa, if not even Chris or Captain Miles suspected Eggleston of being capable of going to such lengths, how can you be expected to? No, I don't blame you for that."

He had a point. That actually hadn't occurred to me before—nor the corollary, which was that perhaps all the scolding I was receiving from Chris, Sapphira, and Tyler was coming from their own guilt at having missed the signs of danger.

"As for the violence," Selby continued. "It makes me sick—absolutely sick—that you were forced to endure that. To do that. I would give all I have on two worlds to have kept that from you."

The passion in his voice, and on his face, shook me. I had no words.

He rubbed his hands through his hair. "You're right that I was acting like a three-year-old instead of your friend. But it wasn't because I was angry at you. It was because I couldn't come near you without wanting to kill Eggleston myself."

"Oh," I said, brilliantly.

"But that wasn't the action of a friend," he said. "Please don't apologize for something that was by no means your fault, Nerissa. I'm the one who is sorry. Forgive me?"

Of course I forgave him, and what's more, I even managed to keep from apologizing for yelling at him as I did so. I wanted to give him a hug, but he's not exactly the hugging type, so instead I walked back to sickbay with him, where we chatted normally about ordinary things for a few more minutes, to Allain's great relief, and then I went on my way to go reassure Chris that my kidnapping was no more her fault than it was mine.

Overall, I'm still a little unsettled from the encounter. It was so much more intense than I ever expected from Selby, of all people. I don't quite know what to make of it.

Day Forty-Seven/October 6, 102.

Chris and I are on good terms again. She broke down into tears—highly alarming—when I told her not to blame herself for letting Egghead get me, and then I think I made things worse when I told her that it was only because of her training that I was able to fight him and gain control of the shuttle. I was *trying* to make things better. Oops. Tyler is back to his ebullient self, and Sapphira "hopes I have learned something from this" and then proceeds as if nothing has happened. Mark is bearing up well under his new role as head scientist, but he took the time to apologize to me for not noticing that his boss was slowly turning homicidal. I reassured him as well, and everything seems back to normal between me and all my friends here. Aside from whatever oddness is going on with Selby. I'm not going to worry about that, though. It's probably just Selby being *Selby*.

The tribunal for Dr. Eggleston starts today. It's highly stiff and formal and militaristic, and I think I'm more nervous about it than Egghead himself. Stupidly enough, I have been sitting here fretting over the fact that I don't have any decent formal clothing to wear to it. I am deeply grateful to Chris for her clothes, but I am getting tired of wearing the same two outfits all the time.

The formal clothing of this day and age is gorgeous, too. It reminds me of styles from Ancient Greece and Egypt, and other Ancient Earth cultures. I wouldn't be wearing any of the flowing, gauzy gowns I've seen on the aether, since those are more *fancy* formal, but it would be nice to have something more impressive to wear to the tribunal than these two casual outfits. Oh well. In the long run, totally not important.

Also not important but an enormous relief to me, all the green is gone. It took the purple out of my hair with it, but Ona said she'd redo that for me whenever I want. I think I'll wait until after the tribunal, since drab brown still says "take me seriously" a little better than electric purple—but as soon as that's done, I'm back to wild color. Maybe it's not as highbrow as keeping one's natural coloring, or even dyeing it a color found in nature, but it's *me*. And that's all that really needs be said about that.

I tried writing poetry earlier this morning, in an attempt to distract myself from everything, but nothing came. Distressing, but not too alarming, given the strain I'm under. I'll be glad when poetry and music can be my default again, though. There's still a gaping hole inside of me where my music used to live, and even if I can find something else on this ship to do, even if I get back to Earth in eight years and build a new life for myself there, I don't think I'll ever feel whole without my music.

Time to go. I haven't seen Dr. Egghead since we got back. Hope I don't throw up all over the place the instant I lay eyes on him.

Day Forty-Eight/October 7, 102.

Great excitement! My little misadventure with Eggleston is behind us and all but forgotten, thanks to this new occurrence. Not any too soon, either. Yesterday was almost worse than the kidnapping was in the first place.

Not really, but whew, talk about stress. They set up a proper tribunal, with Captain Miles and Mark Danvers as magistrates, and conducted a trial for Eggleston. I think I was more of a wreck than he was, frankly. I felt so ridiculously guilty that once more I was putting the ship through something obnoxious and difficult and out-of-the-way of their mission. I'm pretty sure Captain Miles agreed with me, but to do him justice he was angrier with Egghead than with me.

"Whatever inconvenience you may have caused, you did not ask to come here, nor have you deliberately put the crew out to accommodate you more than can be expected from someone of your background," he told me publicly after judgment was passed on Egghead. "It is a discredit on the Alliance that you should have been treated so, and I only hope that this injustice may in time be rectified."

Which is pretty much the nicest thing he's ever said to me.

Both he and Mark worked really hard to come up with a just solution to the problem. If this ship was on a short-term mission, they could have thrown Egghead in the brig and called it good (or, since *Caledonia* doesn't have a brig, confined him to quarters), leaving him for Alliance authorities to deal with. That's not really practical here. Nor is leaving him confined to his quarters for eight years. On the other hand, they can't say "Oh well, we'll let it slide this time, but don't let it happen again."

In his favor is the fact that he did think he was acting in the ship's best interests, and that he never intended to hurt me, only return me to "my people" and warn them off. Against him is the fact that he drugged and abducted me, and snuck around behind the Captain's back instead of handling his concerns in a proper manner.

So, he's confined to quarters for an unconfirmed amount of time, until Captain Miles and Dr. Selby clear him for duty again. He has been fitted with an alarm which will go off if he comes within ten feet of me, or if he attempts to access any ship's operations.

He accepted his punishment with surprising calm. He hasn't apologized to me, but according to Mark he took seriously my suggestion of finding a different hypothesis regarding my arrival on the ship. He doesn't mind being confined to quarters for now, he said, because it will give him a chance to look into the matter.

I still don't trust him any further than I can throw him, and I can't be near him without breaking into a cold sweat, but hopefully by the time he's out and about the ship again, we'll both have recovered. And I don't have to worry about him ever coming close to me again, thanks to the alarm.

It was an awful, horrible experience, even by the standards of what I've seen and done since arriving here, but nobody died, and I'm ready to close the book on it and move on. So is everyone else, I think, which is one reason why we're all so giddy about this.

The "thing" we picked up on long-range sensors, that Egghead thought was a ship or traveling space station belonging to *my people*, is a ship. And we've made contact! This is the first contact they've made with a new species since the mission began. You can imagine how stoked everyone is.

The ship is called the *Xa-Free-Unh*, its captain is Huy-Erh-Lun, and the species are the Martok. That's all we know about them; the Alliance has never encountered this race before. The Captains only spoke together today, tomorrow we will be in close enough range that we'll be able to see them as well as talk (video chat for the modern era!). Sapphira has asked for special permission for me to be tucked away in a corner of the bridge for that, as they are still working on finding What Riss Does Best aboard the ship and she wants to see how I react to First Contact, and also get my impressions of the meeting afterward. Miles was grumpy, but he couldn't exactly refuse. He gave me a reprieve because of the whole kidnapping thing, but now he's getting jumpy again about wrapping things up, so this is Sapphira's last big chance to Prove My Worth. Or something. At any rate ...

I, Nerissa Waldon, am going to be part of a First Contact with an alien species. Never thought I'd write those words.

* * *

Selby, for the first time, joined me for lunch yesterday. I was sitting with Ona and her engineering team again, and as usual, we were discussing music. We've covered instruments fairly thoroughly, and now we were on to styles. The folk music I do so well sounds as quaint and antiquated to them as medieval ballads do to me. Lhude sing cuccu.

Selby didn't join in the conversation, but he didn't exactly cast a pall over it, either: he was just there, sitting on the other side of me from Ona, listening and eating. After he finished he squeezed my shoulder briefly and then went back to sickbay, all without saying one word.

It's like him and yet different, and still very unnerving.

Later.

Mark and Selby knocked on my door a little while ago. I invited them in, although there's really not room for three people comfortably in here.

"I'll be brief," said Mark. "I think we've figured out a temporary solution to your DNA situation."

Would you believe that in all this fuss and pother with Egghead I'd completely forgotten about that?

"Ah," I said. "That."

"Yes," said Mark. "I was working on that before ... well, before the, uh, incident, and I finally hit on the answer this morning."

As he explained it, they don't need to do an operation. They've figured out a way to suppress any reaction between my DNA and the DNA of this universe. I have to give myself a shot (except it's not really a shot, since they don't use needles; I press the not-syringe to my skin and release the trigger, and whatever's inside it absorbs through my skin) every morning.

"Like insulin for diabetes," I said.

"What's that?" Mark asked, and I realized anew the difference in era.

"Ancient disease," Selby said, confirming that. "Long since cured."

"Oh," said Mark, and dismissed it.

"And what about ... children?" I asked, still kind of embarrassed to be talking about this with them. It wouldn't have been so bad except Mark had wanted to date me and Selby has seen me at my most vulnerable, and talking about such intimate matters with them both, together, felt wrong on several levels.

"Time enough to worry about that when it's relevant," Selby said. "There's a very good chance that the difference would not transfer genetically. If it does, we could do a fetal operation to suppress or even remove it. No danger to you or the baby," he added, perhaps seeing the horror on my face. "If the time ever comes when you want to think about having children, we'll talk over the options then."

I looked at the suppression serum. "And ... this isn't going to change me at all. I know it sounds dumb, but—"

"Not dumb at all," Mark said, smiling at me reassuringly. "The answer is no. You'll still be Riss. Just Riss without potential nasty allergic reactions."

"OK then," I said.

They left, and that was that.

For them, anyway. It took me a little while to wrap my brain around the matter being taken care of so easily. Like, shouldn't there be more danger to me involved? Or at least more blood drawn? With all the worry and fretting I did over it, and now it's nothing more than giving myself a not-shot every morning?

I am grateful, and telling myself not to be absurd. There's enough going on to occupy my attention. One less thing to think about is good. And at the bottom of my soul, I am deeply relieved. I'm not going to die if I eat the wrong thing, and I'm not going to become less of myself by taking care of the matter.

One more worry off my mind.

Day Forty-Nine/October 8, 102.

Well.

Well.

Today was the Big Day—First Contact with the Martok people. I felt odd about being on the bridge for it—thrilled, obviously, but I kept thinking about what Captain Miles said to me back when we first talked about me being useful here, about all the people on this ship working for most of their lives for the privilege of being here, and here I was just waltzing onto the bridge for this huge, historic moment without any kind of preparation or effort.

Sapphira gave me an odd little smile when I told her this.

"Look at it this way," she said. "It's not like we're kicking somebody else off the bridge so you can be there. If you didn't come, that corner would be empty."

That did make me feel better.

So there I was, standing unobtrusively in my little corner (metaphorically—the bridge is technically all rounded walls and curves), with the Captain ostentatiously ignoring me, Lieutenant Vreean genuinely ignoring me, Ru El giving me a courteous nod and *then* ignoring me, Sapphira very focused and intense on her work, but occasionally checking back over her shoulder to see how I was doing, and Chris nearly bouncing at her console from excitement.

That last is not poetic license, by the way. I could see from where I was standing—she kept rising up on her toes, and then forcing herself back down, then up again, and down, and so on.

The bridge itself is much more utilitarian than what I was expecting. I hadn't been able to pay that much attention to it the last time I was there—the day we talked to other-Riss. I was a little distracted by God turning my life upside down and shaking it before setting me back on my feet. This time, I took it all in.

While Engineering was cleaner and calmer than I had envisioned, the bridge itself is smaller and more basic. Rounded walls, like I've already said, and low consoles, and viewports on three sides. The Captain's chair is in the middle, raised on a sort of dais so he can oversee everything, and the other stations are in horseshoe shape around it, with the back of the room, by the doors (where I stood) the only empty space.

Sapphira's chair is not next to Miles's. She has her own proper console in the horseshoe, to the right of his chair. Chris's console is on the left, and Helm and Navigation are in the front.

We could see the Martok ship out the viewports. Long and bulbous, like a cigar with blobs. At the appointed time, the central viewscreen changed, showing us our first Martok.

He was humanoid, two arms and two legs, one head, features arranged where they would be on human face. Bronze skin—not metallic, like Tyler's skin, but a warm, natural looking golden-brown. Dark green eyes, red mouth pierced by several rings, a flat nose, eyebrows winging off toward his ears with more rings hanging from them, wide ears with yet more piercings, and pale yellow hair pulled up into a topknot. He wore these wicked cool dark purple leather pants—nice and tight, we could all see he had a great rear—and a black leather vest with no shirt underneath. His arms were *ripped*.

He had a broadsword, no joke, strapped across his back, and a ray-gun of sorts holstered at his waist, and knives were strapped to his legs. I'm not entirely certain, but I'm pretty sure the silver thing holding his topknot in place was a stiletto blade.

The rest of the crew on their bridge looked fairly similar, and the bridge itself was dark, with flashing silver and blue lights running constantly across the panels. All in all, it looked wildly barbaric in comparison with the strict simplicity and neatness of Captain Miles and his crew.

It also looked *freaking awesome*. Space warriors. Johnny Depp would have *loved* playing Huy-Erh-Lun in a movie.

"I greet you," Captain Miles said in his stiff, stilted way. "In the name of the Earth Alliance. As I said when we spoke earlier, I am Captain Arthur Miles of the Alliance Exploratory Fleet space corvette *Caledonia*. We are a peaceful people, hoping to extend the hand of friendship to all alien peoples we may encounter ..."

And so on. I could have told him he was doing it *all wrong*. First of all, you don't talk about "alien peoples" when you are the alien one in this part of space. Second, what if "extending the hand" means something totally different to this culture than it does in ours? I mean, everyone in my day knows not to make the "V for Victory" sign in certain countries. You'd think a spaceship captain would know better. This is why they need diplomats!

I watched Huy-Erh-Lun closely as the Captain droned on, and I knew we were heading for trouble. His initial posture—legs spread a normal width apart, hands down and open at his sides, head level—spoke of alertness and caution, but not danger. As soon as Captain Miles mentioned "peaceful people," everything changed. His feet spread a bit more, his fists clenched before his hands moved to the small of his back, and his head reared back while his upper lip raised in a sneer.

Finally, Miles shut up and gave him a chance to reply.

"I am the warrior Huy-Erh-Lun," he said. "I have the incomprehensible honor to be in charge of this noble vessel on its voyage. I represent the Martok people in this, our first meeting between your Earth Alliance and the honorable Martok."

Honor, noble, honorable. A person doesn't throw those words around that much in a short time without it being significant.

"We would very much like to learn more about the Martok, Captain Huy-Erh-Lun," Miles said, which was another mistake. If Huy-Erh-Lun didn't call himself a Captain, Miles shouldn't have either. "And for you to learn more of us. Perhaps we could discuss a mutually beneficial alliance between our peoples?" Way to rush into things. Maybe learn more about the people first, *then* discuss an alliance?

Now Huy-Erh-Lun stiffened even more. "You are so eager to join with every ship you meet?"

Captain Miles spread his hands. "We wish friendship with all peoples."

"The Martok are, perhaps, more discerning. We do not distribute friendship indiscriminately, but choose only those who are worthy."

"It is my hope that you will find the Earth Alliance worthy," said Captain Miles.

Huy-Erh-Lun sneered. " am sure you do." And he cut the connection.

The discussion that went on around the bridge after that was interesting, to say the least. Chris wanted to call for Action Stations, for fear the Martok would attack the ship. Sapphira didn't go that far, but it was clear she didn't think the exchange had gone well. Ru El believed the situation could be redeemed, and that the Martok people might be of great value to the Alliance, once properly cultivated. Lieutenant Vreean ignored everyone else. Tyler chimed in via com from Engineering, leaning toward Ru El's point of view.

Captain Miles declared that the Martok people were obviously savage barbarians, and could be A) of no value to the Alliance, and B) no danger to the ship. His military background was a real hindrance here. Sapphira had to remind him that the mission was to connect with as many new peoples as possible, regardless of our own personal opinions, before he would grumpily agree to try again.

Ru El opened the com again. "Captain Huy-Erh-Lun," Miles said, while I winced in my corner. "I'm afraid we got off on the wrong foot." (Again with the Earth-English metaphors!) "I would like to invite you, and any members of your crew you wish to bring along, to come aboard the *Caledonia* and dine with my senior staff and me, in hopes of getting to know each other better."

The viewscreen flashed back to life and we got to see Huy-Erh-Lun in all his magnificent sneer-ness. "You allow strangers aboard your ship, Alliance captain?"

"We have nothing to fear," said Captain Miles. "Nor should you fear any harm from us."

That was his biggest mistake of all. Huy-Erh-Lun's face went maroon, and without him saying anything at all to his crew, they powered up weapons and very obviously prepared to fire on us.

"Shield—" Chris squeaked. She cleared her throat and tried again. "Shield at maximum, Captain. Call to Action Stations?"

He nodded, and she hit the ship-wide intercom.

"All hands, Action Stations!" she shouted. The lights on the bridge dimmed, and a low, moaning klaxon came on in the background.

"Power up the weapons, but do not fire unless I say so," Miles told her. He turned back to the viewscreen, still on. "Captain, are you getting ready to attack us?"

"Give me a reason not to!" Huy-Erh-Lun roared.

"Because we will destroy you," snapped Miles.

That was not the reason the Martok wanted.

Their guns fired, splashing crimson against our shield, surrounding the *Caledonia* with a red halo.

"Direct hit," Vreean said calmly. "No damage."

"Should I shoot back?" Chris asked, nearly dancing with agitation.

"I said not until I give the order, Commander," Miles barked. "Helm, take evasive action."

Xa-Free-Unh fired again, and again, and then twisted up and above us. *Caledonia* shuddered under the attack, but so far, thanks to Ru El's skillful piloting, the shield held.

"They're coming around to attack from behind," Ru El announced.

I couldn't take it any longer. I did some hopping up and down of my own, hoping to get Sapphira's attention. Instead, the Captain turned and looked at me.

"Commander Osei-Koné, take your protege off the bridge at once!"

She stood up. "Come on, Riss," she said, and we exited together. "My fault," she said as the doors closed. "I forgot to tell you that you'd need to leave for your quarters or sickbay if the captain called for Action Stations."

I didn't even care. "Sapphira, they think he insulted them. That's why they attacked. Didn't you hear Huy-Erh-Lun going on and on about honor? And his stuffiness at the idea of friendship with just anyone? They're obviously a people who value their personal and cultural honor incredibly highly, and when the captain suggested they might be afraid of us, they took it as a deadly insult. The crew didn't even wait for Huy-Erh-Lun to give the order before they prepared to attack us!"

Sapphira gave me the full blast of her intense stare. I staggered and tried not to reel backward.

"What do you think we should do?"

"Apologize," I said at once. "But don't grovel. Tell them you did not mean to offend, that it was caused by your own ignorance, and that you can now see that the noble Martok—or something like that—would never have to fear anyone."

"Then we can suggest that if both sides agree to a truce, nobody has to lose honor by surrendering," she mused, eyes now fixed on the corridor wall.

"Yes, and see if there's a neutral place you can meet, so that nobody has to go to the other's ship," I said. "Tell them you want to learn about the Martok so you can give them the full respect they so clearly deserve, and that you hope they are able to respect our culture once they learn about us."

She fixed her eyes on me again. "Stay there," she said, and vanished back onto the bridge again.

I waited as ordered, trying to keep my footing as the ship took three more hits. I began to fear that either tMiles hadn't listened to Sapphira, or that I'd been entirely wrong, when the shooting stopped, and the alert level lowered to stand-by.

I dared breathe again. Had it worked?

The door to the bridge opened again. Sapphira grinned at me.

"Nice work, Riss," she said. "Hope you don't mind. I volunteered you to be part of the landing party to meet the Martok."

Well!

Day Fifty-One/October 10, 102.

I am not supposed to be writing at all. Selby has threatened to break my pen and burn my journal if he catches me, but if I don't at least start writing this down now, I'll forget half of it.

Lieutenant Allain is obligingly blocking me from the Doc's view, and I will write as much as I can before he has to move and Selby can see me again.

So, Day Fifty, yesterday. The Martok had agreed to meet our party at a nearby uninhabited moon (orbiting a gas giant, but with breathable atmosphere. Not, alas, a forest moon). Along with Sapphira and me, our team consisted of two Security officers, Mark Danvers (representing the scientists), Ensign Carr, and a young Arethran lieutenant who piloted the shuttle.

My breathing quickened a little as I entered the shuttle, but other than that instinctive fear, I had no other flashbacks to my little misadventure with Egghead (little, ha ha). And once we were settled down inside, I focused on deep breathing and thinking about what was to come, and soon enough the tightness in my chest eased and I could breathe comfortably again.

The Martok arrived at the moon almost the same time we did (which makes sense, when you think about it, since we left at the same time from relatively the same place). Only five of them, including Huy-Erh-Lun, all looking like major kick-ass alien warriors.

I had only been with *Caledonia* a few days when I went to Planet Hell. This time, stepping out of the shuttle and onto *terra firma* was almost enough to make me burst into tears. It was so good—amazingly good—to walk on real ground again, not ship's floors, and to breathe real, fresh, slightly-stinky air instead of recycled oxygen.

The moon was nothing at all like ours. Gravity was maybe a little lighter—my steps felt buoyant, but I didn't go floating off into the air with each step. Tall, green, rubbery-looking frond-things grew from the ground and waved in the air, and here and there were puddles of red water. The ground itself was red-and-yellow streaked, with piles of yellow rocks lumped up all over. My second alien world, and it was as alien to Planet

Hell as it was to Earth-as-I-knew-it. Much less stark and terrifying than Planet Hell, thank goodness. The last thing we needed was a fiery wave to engulf us all in the midst of negotiations.

"Greetings," Sapphira called as we all walked to a central flat space between the two shuttles. "I am Commander Sapphira Osei-Koné." She introduced the rest of us, ending with, "And this is Nerissa Waldon, our Cultural Expert and Diplomatic Envoy. She will be speaking for our party."

I've never been sucker-punched or had my legs kicked out from under me (though Egghead came close), but just then I knew exactly how both of those would feel. At the same time.

(Afterward, she explained that it was totally an impulse of the moment, and apologized, but her mouth kept twitching as she did so so I don't exactly believe her.)

I couldn't turn and run, or throw up, so I stepped forward and gave a little half-bow, which felt right at the time but probably looked completely stupid. "It is a great honor to meet such noble beings as yourselves. I can only feel sorrow that we have never heard of the mighty Martok people before now, and hope that before long, we can speak of your greatness to all the stars."

I dared look up. The alien members of *Caledonia's* crew look normal to me now, and Huy-Erh-Lun didn't look that odd through the viewport, but seeing him in person, up close, he seemed so utterly *other* that my throat closed and I had to struggle to keep from complete panic.

Then he smiled, and it's true what they say, that a smile is universal. More like multi-universal, because my panic eased at once. Granted, the many piercings in his lips and his pointed teeth made the smile look more like a leer, but still. I stopped worrying that he was going to snap me in two.

"And I greet you, Nerissa Waldon, and your people," Huy-Erh-Lun said. "We also have never heard of this Earth Alliance. I am sorry to tell you that our impression of you is not so favorable as yours of us."

"I fear there was a great deal of misunderstanding at our last encounter," I agreed. "I deeply regret that."

Then we all sat down on the ground and I didn't have to do all the talking, though Sapphira refused to take command, and Mark followed her lead, the traitor (good thing we *weren't* dating, or I would've had to break up with him for that).

The Martok are, as I surmised, an honor-based society. Most honor comes from war, naturally, but also in art, creating great beauty of any sort (this doesn't just mean drawing/painting type of art, but music, poetry, gardening, any sort of creative act). And no matter what one's calling is, self-sacrifice for the good of others is the highest honor anyone could achieve.

Aside from the war thing, I kind of like the sound of their society. A world where artists are held in higher regard than almost anyone else? Sign me up, man.

Huy-Erh-Lun didn't come right out and say this, but I got the impression that their species is often mistaken for bloodthirsty savages, as the Captain assumed about them, and very few ever bother looking past the warriors to see the artists.

That was when Sapphira said, "Nerissa is an artist."

My face burned, and all the Martok looked at me with potential respect.

"I am a musician," I said. "Though I have not made music in more than a year."

"A creator who abandons her calling is worse than one who never hears its call to begin with," Huy-Erh-Lun said. "I begin to perceive that your people are as empty of honor as I suspected." He spat on the ground.

It only occurred to me later that I should have been upset that we were losing an alliance and might end up getting killed by the Martok for being honorless. At that moment, I was only furious over the aspersion cast on my passion.

"I abandoned nothing," I said in a tight voice. Mark told me afterward my eyes went hard as flint and my face was completely white, and he'd never been so terrified of anyone in his entire life. I suspect he exaggerates, but yes. I was freaking pissed. "My heart shattered when my husband—my life's partner [I had no idea if they had the concept of marriage in their culture] died. One cannot make art when one's soul contains nothing but grief. And now that I have begun to heal, I am here in this place without my instrument, and no matter how devoted one is to one's craft, one cannot create without the tools!"

Huy-Erh-Lun placed his hands flat on his knees and bowed his head, followed by the other four warriors. "I spoke in ignorance of your loss."

Sapphira placed her hand on my shoulder. "It is true that we of the Earth Alliance are not renowned for honor, as the Martok are. Rather, we are known and respected for our curiosity, our passion for scientific knowledge. We do not war for the sake of glory; we fight only to defend ourselves, when we've no other options. But that does not mean we are without honor entirely, that we will not fight to defend what we hold valuable, nor that we do not give the creative gifts their proper due. We pursue knowledge for the sake of science, but we also appreciate beauty. And perhaps a friendship with your people would help us respect it even more."

Huy-Erh-Lun was silent. Then he said, "I will consider your words. If you can prove them."

Sapphira spread her hands. "Try us."

He looked at me. "Describe your instrument to me.'

In halting words, I explained an acoustic guitar, and then spoke a little bit about pianos. He nodded.

"We have a very similar instrument to your *kitar* [that was the closest he could get to "guitar" even through the translator]. I, in fact, have one on board my ship. It belonged to my sister, who was killed in battle defending her young ones, and whose name is immortalized in the Halls of our Dead. If you, playing this, can prove your devotion to your art, we will consider an alliance."

"And if she fails the test?" Mark said, clearing his throat and speaking for the first time.

Huy-Erh-Lun's eyes were implacable. "Then we shall consider you liars and barbarians, and shall look upon the Earth Alliance as our enemy."

"Oh good," I said faintly. "No pressure."

(Ah crap. Selby just noticed me writing.)

Day Fifty-Two/October 11, 102.

Selby nearly turned purple yesterday when he caught me writing on the sly.

"What's that?" he said. "Allain, you were supposed to be watching her!"

I shoved this book and my pen under my pillow. "What's what? I'm just innocently resting here until you clear me to return to my quarters. Right, Allain?"

(Poor Allain.)

"That clearance will come *never* if you keep blatantly going against my orders!" Selby said. He stormed over to the bed and tried to rip the pillow away to get at the journal beneath.

I kept a firm grip on it, and we had a beautiful tug-of-war with the entire medical staff watching. Allain got his revenge by collecting bets.

"I ... don't ... think ... this is good ... for my ... fingers," I gritted.

"Then ... let ... go!" he said.

"You're the doctor, you're supposed to do what's best for the patient," I said.

"What's best for this patient is a swift kick in the—"

Which is, of course, when Captain Miles walked in.

But what *he* had to say isn't going to make any sense until I finish writing out what happened two days ago. Which I can do now, because I'm enough better that I am allowed to write for ten minutes at a time, with ten minute breaks in between.

Selby is totally making me do this for his own amusement. There *cannot* be medical sense behind it.

So. Back to the not-forest moon.

Sapphira tried to argue with Huy-Erh-Lun, but he remained obdurate. In fact, the more she argued, the more conditions he set. He said that I had to play something I composed myself, words *and* music, or it would be meaningless.

Sapphira was ready to give up the entire thing, fight the Martok right then and there to get us back to the *Caledonia*, and then go to battle with their ship, and Mark kept trying to think of an alternative, when I stepped in.

"I'll do it," I told them. The Martok had withdrawn a few paces to give us privacy to discuss our decision.

"Riss, you don't have to prove yourself to us," Sapphira said. "You don't have to prove yourself to *them*."

"And you certainly don't have to put yourself at risk like this for us," Mark said.

"Thank you," I said, and meant it. "But please, let me at least try. Not to—not to prove anything. But to try to do something good for you guys, who have done so much for me."

And to my astonishment, they exchanged glances with each other, and stepped back to let me tell Huy-Erh-Lun that I accepted his challenge.

Huy-Erh-Lun sent someone back to his ship for the *laira*, the guitar-like instrument, while Sapphira called the Captain and updated him on our status. The Martok warrior returned with the instrument, and Huy-Erh-Lun handed it to me.

A laira is more like a square mandolin than a guitar, with a small, boxy body, carved top, and eight strings, but it was easy enough to figure out. The problem was that it had been fifty days since I had picked up a stringed instrument, and had only played a few chords once in a while for a year before that. My calluses were gone, my fingering was rusty, I had no lyrics, and I was trying to prove I could create something beautiful on an alien instrument, with our lives on the line.

Great.

"I'll need some time," I told Huy-Erh-Lun.

"You have twelve hours," he answered.

"Agreed," I said, figuring by the time I'd played for twelve hours I'd either have come up with something genius or keeled over from frustration and bloody fingers. "And one more thing," I added. "If I fail, and you decide we are liars and barbarians, you let the *Caledonia* and her crew leave Martok space peacefully, provided they agree to never return to trouble you again. You can have me, to make your point, but let them go."

He peered at me, and finally nodded. "Acceptable. If you cannot create, you die, but they will have their cowardly lives."

The Martok honored self-sacrifice above all else, even battle glory. If I couldn't convince him of our worthiness by my music, maybe my offering myself up for them would make him think twice about writing us off. It took some of the pressure off, at least.

I wasn't scared of dying. Andrew's death had broken me; my own, after that, seemed little more than another step along the path. Since coming to this universe I had started appreciating my life more, but death was still a familiar and comfortable concept. I would hate not getting a chance to know the rest of the crew, to deepen my friendships with those I already did know, to miss out on all the exciting discovering they were going to make.

But at least they would still be alive to make those discoveries, instead of dead because I got a bad case of stage fright.

Argh, writing it down makes it look all soppy no matter how I put it. Let me rephrase: it would suck to die, but not as much as it would suck if all of us died.

I went off to a quiet corner of the moon (fine, a yellow rocky spot a few feet away from the landing area) and started strumming.

Two hours later, I was still strumming.

Two hours after that, I was ...

By the time six hours had passed, I was convinced I had blown it. My music was gone, I had lost it through neglect, and now I had nothing but enormously painful fingers, cramped hands, and an empty mind to offer anyone. Maybe Huy-Erh-Lun had been right about me.

Sapphira came to make me take a break (I still don't know what exactly the rest of them did while I practiced. Played poker in the shuttle, I suppose).

"I'm sorry I got you into this," she said, handing me a water tube and a protein square. "I had no idea, when I told them you were an artist, that it would lead to ... this. I know you said you're willing to do this, but I've still tried talking him out of this, not because I don't believe you can do it, but because it's completely unfair to you. I even told him everything about how you got here and how we can't expect this much from you right now, but he won't listen. Told me that you accepted the challenge, and now we must abide by the rules."

She grabbed my head between her two hands. "But we will not let them kill you if you can't write a song. Don't think that for even one minute. Captain Miles wants to give you a chance to succeed, but we're not going to fly off and leave you here to them if you fail. You are part of the *Caledonia* now. We don't leave our people behind."

It was terribly unfair of her to tell me that when my mouth was full of dry protein square and I couldn't even cry.

"Oh, and the Doc says he's going to lock you up and throw away the key when we get back," she added. "For being so stupid to agree to this in the first place."

I swallowed and managed to cover up my tears with a laugh. "He's mad?" Poor Selby. I keep doing this to him.

"First time I've ever seen him argue with the Captain in *favor* of violence. Tyler sends his love, says you'll knock their socks off, or whatever the Martok equivalent of socks are, and Chris is about ready to commandeer a shuttle and attempt a rescue of you all on her own, except she'd have half the crew coming with her, making it something more than a solo attempt." She smiled at me, that brilliant, glittering smile that makes everyone, including me, adore her. "I'm with Tyler. I believe you can do this. But if you can't, don't worry. We've got your back."

She left me to my work, and I could breathe again.

I'd gotten it all wrong. I'd been so focused on the medium. I thought I had to write a good song, a great song, the best song ever, or Huy-Erh-Lun would declare me incompetent and kill me and try to kill my friends.

But that's never been why I play. I create for the joy within me, to share that joy with others. I create because it is my way of giving some beauty back to the One who made the universe so beautiful. And I create for love.

It's not the medium. Sometimes it's not even the message. Sometimes, it's all about the one who receives it, the one—or ones—for whom I create.

An hour after that, I walked over to Huy-Erh-Lun.

"I need to thank you," I told him.

He blinked a few times. "Thank me?"

"This is the song I've needed to write for the last several weeks, but I couldn't get it out. I was too distracted, and it was trapped inside of me. Now it's freed, and it is thanks to you." I bowed, sat down, and began to play.

I was lost and alone
In the darkness, no place to call my home
I was blinded by sorrow and need
There was no hope, no light I could see

Then love came and lifted me
Took me from my place of grief, brought me to my knees
Out of the darkness and into the light
Away from the shadows into a day so bright

Now I'm here and it's new
Still I'm scared, don't know what to do
Everything changed, nothing is the same
Except for love, that will always remain

For love came and lifted me
Took me from my place of grief, brought me to my knees
Out of the darkness and into the light
Away from the shadows into a day so bright

No longer alone, I'm not lost anymore
I've come through my grief, passed through that door
The past is behind me, complete, it is done
My heart's full of joy, a new life's begun

* * *

For love came and lifted me
Took me from my place of grief, brought me to my knees
Out of the darkness and into the light
Away from the shadows into a day so bright

I'm not home, but I'm where I'm meant to be
It's not home, but this is where I'm meant to be.

I didn't find out until afterward that Sapphira broadcast the performance back to the ship, and they played it over the entire com system, so *everyone* heard it.

I managed to sing the entire thing, but when I played the chorus without words one final time at the end, the tears started pouring down my face. By the time I lifted my still-bleeding fingers from the final chord, I was a weepy mess, like I haven't been in ages. And despite my old discomfort with being emotional in front of others, I didn't care.

I ignored Huy-Erh-Lun and turned to Sapphira. "Thank you," I said thickly.

She nodded, her own eyes suspiciously bright.

I stood and held the laira out to Huy-Erh-Lun. He also stood, following by the rest of his warriors. He ignored the laira, drew one of his knives, and closed his hand around its hilt, blade pointing downward.

I was sure he would say I failed, and then stab me in the heart.

Instead, he went down on one knee, and crossed the fist holding the knife over his chest, holding it right above where a human's heart is.

"I honor you," he said, and his warriors all followed suit.

I lost any breath I had left over that.

Then Mark, over on our side, slipped to one knee and held his right fist over his heart. Ensign Carr did it next, and before I knew it they were all kneeling, even Sapphira.

I shook my head. "You've got it all wrong," I said. "If I have done anything worthy of honor at all, it is only because it was given to me first."

Sapphira shook her head right back at me. "You're the one who's got it wrong, Riss. You've had that honor from the beginning. You just needed somebody to show you."

Things moved quickly after that. We took the shuttle back to the *Caledonia*, where Selby dragged me off to sickbay to bandage my fingers and yell at me. Sapphira and Captain Miles hammered out a tentative alliance treaty with Huy-Erh-Lun on behalf of the Martok. We are not, as I understand it, formally allies, but we will do our best to assist each other when needed. Friends with benefits, I call it.

(Tyler cracked up at that one. He came to see me almost as soon as I reached sickbay, beaming and proud. "I knew you could do it," he said. "The rest of them, they were all panicking, but I said, Nah, Riss'll pull it off. Just watch. And was I ever right!" He kissed my cheek and told me to get some rest, and then Selby kicked him out.)

And now I can write what Captain Miles said to me when he walked in on Selby and me fighting over the pillow.

"I have reviewed your evaluation reports from Commander Tyler, Commander Osei-Koné, and Doctor Selby," he said, as though he hadn't just seen the two of us behaving like a couple of five-year-olds. "As well as Commander Osei-Koné's report from the Martok incident. All three of the evaluations agreed that since you came on board, you have gotten to know more of the crew members than many officers have since our mission began. Not only have you taken the time to meet them, you have interested yourself in them and learned about them, about their cultures and about their characters, their personalities, their hopes and fears. You have also studied, on your own account, without anyone suggesting to you it would be a good thing, the history of the last 510 years, and the cultures of many of the alien worlds we know.

"Commander Osei-Koné also noted, for the Martok incident, that your relative lack of prejudice regarding alien species and your ability to see beyond the surface of a situation to get at the subtleties of a matter were extremely useful in allowing us to avoid a battle with their ship. Your willingness to sacrifice yourself for the chance to ally with the Martok, as well as save the lives aboard this ship that would surely have been lost even in a victorious battle, speaks for itself.

"In short, Ms. Waldon, I am confirming Commander Osei-Koné's informal designation of you as Cultural Expert and Diplomatic Envoy. Your tasks will involve interacting with the crew to keep their spirits up each according to their own way, as well as accompanying any First Contacts and other meetings with new civilizations, to share your insights with myself and the commander. We will give you an office, where the members of this crew can come and talk to you when they need, and where you can continue your studies into the peoples of this galaxy. Your duties will begin once Doctor Selby clears you for active service."

He hesitated. "You are not a member of the Fleet, nor even of the Alliance, unless at some point you wish to swear an oath to them. But I believe you will, in time, become a valued member of this crew, for this mission."

Which is about as nice as Captain Miles will ever get. I was genuinely touched.

So. Now I've a place among the crew. Doing, pretty much, exactly what I was already doing, except now with a couple fancy official titles to go along with it (I am already thinking of how I want to be addressed. Ms. Waldon is getting old. I like Your Excellency, or Your Worship, or Great and Glorious Riss. Selby advised me to keep thinking). I have an office in addition to my cabin. I have a paycheck, since Earth has confirmed my official-unofficial status, which means that if we ever land on a planet with CLOTHING FOR SALE I can give Chris back her wardrobe. I have a musical instrument, since Huy-Erh-Lun told me to keep his sister's laira and play it in her honor.

I kept saying all along how important an ambassador of sorts was to this sort of mission. I hope AEF Command takes note, and starts assigning actual, real diplomats to future missions, instead of leaving them as afterthoughts. I am going to study like mad so that next time we come across a situation like the Martok incident, I don't have to wing it. But at least I know what I'm doing now. I have a purpose.

Most importantly, I have a family of sorts. I have friends.

And that's enough for me, for now.

In fact, it's more than enough.

Day Sixty/October 19, 102.

I am sitting in my new office. It's tiny, of course—they cleared some junk out of the smallest cargo bay for me, and the crew in engineering built me this fantastically ugly (but awesome) desk out of damaged parts, and Ensign Carr stole the only comfortable chair from mess for me (I have a couple less-comfortable chairs for when people come to visit). Chris put some picture-projections on my walls, all nature scenes from Earth, Arethra, and a couple other planets. Tyler is working on creating a long window seat to go beneath my viewport, since he knows how much I love the little one in my cabin.

Sapphira contributed a tall, narrow, abstract sculpture that she said they were given on a planet they visited seven months ago and nobody knew what to do with. We put it in the opposite corner from where my laira is stored, and the two alien pieces balance each other nicely. Mark gave me a self-heating kettle and a box of tea and coffee sachets so I can make hot drinks whenever I want (I promptly said "Tea. Earl Grey. Hot," when he handed it to me, and nobody understood why I then went off into gales of laughter).

Lieutenant Allain and the rest of the med staff presented me with a journal-tablet and stylus for when this one runs out, and laughed themselves sick when the Doc started to sputter incoherently.

Dr. Egghead (I accidentally called him that in front of Mark, who choked and then went into spasms of laughter) sent an official message that he has decided I am *not* a danger to the ship after all, but he still doesn't like me. He's still confined to quarters, so I don't really care, but again, it's nice to have that nastiness wrapped up.

Captain Miles even stopped by after we had all worked for a day to get the office fixed up, nodded, and left, which I consider a win. So overall I'm feeling pretty on top of the world.

My photo of Andrew is still in my cabin, a personal, private memory. My wedding ring is now sitting next to it. I think it's time to—not forget, never that, but to move forward with this life I have now. On this desk, I have a still of all of us: Chris, Sapphira, Tyler, Mark, Ona, Carr, Allain, all the rest who helped me put together this office, and me in the middle. Part of my new family.

Selby dropped by after everyone else had gone, and I was sitting flipping through the pages of this journal.

"I should have spaced that thing when we first pulled you on board," he grumbled.

"Why does it bother you so much?" I asked, genuinely curious.

He leaned forward in his chair. "The truth? It worried me at first, how you put on a calm face in front of everyone else, and then gave in to your emotions in a book. Then it just annoyed me."

I set it back down. "Then you'll be glad to know I'm done with it."

He raised his eyebrows. "Really?"

I nodded. "I had already decided. I don't need it anymore." I relaxed and laced my fingers together atop my head. "I don't trust people easily. Especially with my heart, especially after Andrew died. And so at first, the journal was the place I could be *me*, without fear of getting trampled or broken."

I took a deep breath. "But I do trust you now. Sapphira, Chris, Tyler ... you. You probably most, because you got me through some of my worst moments at the beginning, even though I know that was just you being a doctor, and because I know I can always be honest with you without judgement. I don't need to hide behind paper."

He was quiet for a moment. Then,

"It wasn't just being a doctor," he said. "Not once. Not even at the beginning. And it certainly isn't now."

And that was that.

I don't know what exactly he meant by that. I have my suspicions, but I'm not going to dwell on them. I don't know what's going to happen down the road. I don't know much about anything, really, but I'm all right with that.

I'm not home, but this is where I'm meant to be.

The End

Acknowledgements

No man is an island, and no author is, either. So many people helped to shape From the Shadows into what it is today. Many thanks to Angelika, critique partner and beta reader *par excellence*. Some day in Great Britain, dear friend! Thanks also to Laura, editor and encourager, who heroically worked on this even with a newborn. To my beta readers: Amy (without whose plea to turn the Riss novella into a novel this book would not exist); Charolette; Megan; and Livia. Enormous thanks go to Amanda of Fly Casual, who designed the stunning cover and put up with my thousand persnickety alterations. To the friends, family, and neighbors who understood my occasional vanishing from society and put up with my glazed expression as I plotted even in the midst of get-togethers. Most especially to Carl and our girls, who endured late meals, interrupted schooling, distracted mamma/wife, and all the frustrations and joys involved in birthing a book, and who did so graciously and with love.

This book was born out of love for science fiction, space opera, and ordinary people thrust into extraordinary circumstances; it grew into a tribute to light, love, and joy. Thank you to all who do your bit to share those traits with the world; this book is for you: light-bringers, love-pourers, joy-singers.

About the Author

E.L. Bates is the author of the cozy mystery-fantasy *Magic Most Deadly* and, under the name Louise Bates, the upcoming middle grade historical novel *Rivers Wide*. She lives on the beautiful North Shore of Massachusetts with her husband and two daughters. In between homeschooling and writing, she enjoys knitting, quilting, exploring the local beaches and hiking trails with her family, and always, always reading. She is most often found with a cup of tea in hand and dark chocolate close by. *From the Shadows* is her first venture into science fiction. You can find out more about her at her website, http://www.stardancepress.com, or by following her on Twitter @E_L_Bates.

Made in the USA
Middletown, DE
16 February 2016